THE TESLA PARADOX
FOO FIGHTERS

BOOKS BY LAWRENCE ROWE

FICTION

The Founding Fathers Return

NONFICTION

Bubblenomics

Bubblenomics 2

SATIRE

Another Modest Proposal

VISIT LAWRENCE ONLINE

LawrenceRowe.com

THE TESLA PARADOX
FOO FIGHTERS

Lawrence Rowe

New York

Printed in the United States of America by MDR Press.

ISBN-13: 978-0-9767668-6-5

The Tesla Paradox may be purchased at special bulk quantity discounts for educational or promotional use. For information, e-mail: specialmarkets@lawrencerowe.com.

First paperback printing: January 2017.

10   9   8   7   6   5   4   3   2   1

The Tesla Paradox is fiction, but the tens of thousands of bomber and fighter crews that risked their lives in World War II are real. This book is dedicated to their courage and sacrifice.

"The fact that an opinion has been widely held is no evidence whatever that it is not utterly absurd; indeed, in view of the silliness of the majority of mankind, a widespread belief is more likely to be foolish than sensible."

—Bertrand Russell

"A belief may be larger than a fact."

—Vannevar Bush

CONTENTS

FOO FIGHTERS

Floating Silver Balls Latest Nazi Weapons

PARIS, Dec. 13.—(AP)—As the allied armies ground out new gains on the western front today, the Germans were disclosed to have thrown a new "device" into the war—mysterious silvery balls which float in the air.

Pilots report seeing these objects, both individually and in clusters, during forays over the reich.

(The purpose of the floaters was not immediately evident. It is possible that they represent a new anti-aircraft defense instrument or weapon.)

(This dispatch was heavily censored at supreme headquarters.)

Secret Weapon Resembles Yule Decoration

PARIS (INS)—The Germans on the western front have produced a "secret" weapon in keeping with the Christmas season, it was disclosed officially Wednesday.

The new device, apparently an air defense weapon, resembles the huge glass balls which adorn Christmas trees.

They hang in the air sometimes singly, sometimes in clusters. They are colored silver and other shades and are apparently transparent.

No information was available as to what holds them up like stars in the sky, what is in them, or to their purpose.

Lately, they have been seen several times floating over German territory.

Floating Silver Balls Latest Nazi Weapons

Paris Dec. 13, (AP) -- As the Allied armies ground out new gains on the western front today, the Germans were disclosed to have thrown a new "device" into the war -- mysterious silvery balls which float in the air.

Pilots report seeing these objects, both individually and in clusters, during forays over the Reich.

(The purpose of the floaters was not immediately evident. It is possible that they represent a new anti-aircraft defense instrument or weapon.)

(This dispatch was heavily censored at supreme headquarters.)

Secret Weapon Resembles Yule Decoration

PARIS (INS) -- The Germans on the western front have produced a "secret" weapon in keeping with the Christmas season, it was disclosed officially Wednesday.

The new device, apparently an air defense weapon, resembles the huge glass balls which adorn Christmas trees.

They hang in the air sometimes singly, sometimes in clusters. They are colored silver and other shades and are apparently transparent.

No information was available as to what holds them up like stars in the sky, what is in them, or to their purpose.

Lately, they have been seen several times floating over German territory.

Secret Nazi Weapon May Explain Drive

Eisenhower Reported Aware of Inventions Designed to Prolong War

(EDITOR'S NOTE — An illuminating insight into the difficulties confronting the Allied armies in Belgium and possibly explaining the German success to date as a direct result of secret weapons whose nature has not yet been fully divulged is provided in the following delayed dispatch from Paris. It was written on Dec. 16 presumably just a few hours before Nazi Field Marshall Karl Gerd von Rundstedt opened his counteroffensive, but was cleared by censorship to arrive in New York only today.)

By Kingsbury Smith

PARIS, Dec. 16. — (INS) — (Delayed) — The European war is developing today into a race between the Allied offense against Germany, and the perfection of Nazi secret weapons.

There is no doubt that the potential threat of the development of Germany's secret weapons on a large scale is spurting the Allied high command to force a decision as rapidly as possible.

Were it not for the danger of these secret weapons, it is possible that the Allied high command would, in view of the deplorable weather on the Western front, await more favorable conditions before pressing for the final military showdown with the German armies in the west.

However, the possibility that these new weapons, such as the rocket shells, mysterious silver balls, and jet propelled fighter planes, might be produced by the Germans next summer on a scale that might affect Allied military operations is believed to be prompting Gen. Dwight D. Eisenhower to maintain the utmost pressure on the western front despite the worst weather conditions Europe has experienced in 80 years.

There is no thought in Allied military circles that these weapons of the future can save Germany from defeat at this late date. The Nazi war effort has been too greatly crippled for any such miracle to occur. However, the possibility is taken into account that if the Germans could produce these weapons on a large scale they might succeed in prolonging the conflict.

The appearance of a large number of jet-propelled fighter planes with a speed ranging over 600 miles per hour might well reduce the present overwhelming Allied superiority in the air.

Miserable weather conditions have slowed up Gen. Eisenhower's grand scale offensive to smash through the Siegfried line and cross the Rhine. Extraordinary heavy rains, flooded land, mud, and mountain cloud banks have proved an invaluable ally to Germany in this winter campaign.

The most optimistic now dare not hope for the defeat of Germany before the end of February and more conservative observers forsee the European war going well into the summer.

1

Pilot Norb Ostrye peered out the cockpit of the *Bachelor's Den* and scanned the sky, as he had been for hours. Relaxing for five or ten seconds was the natural human inclination, but this was enough time for a pack of Fucking Wolves—German Focke-Wulf fighters—to ambush a B-17 bomber and shoot it down. Ostrye had seen dozens of bombers downed because they hadn't sighted attacking fighters quickly enough. He would never kill his crew with such negligence.

The four 1,200 horsepower Cyclone engines roared steadily, which comforted Ostrye, but they also vibrated the aircraft, which made the long flight grueling. Ostrye envied the freedom of movement of the waist gunners in the rear of the fuselage. He pictured himself standing, touching his toes, the blissful pops and cracks of his scrunched spine as it stretched out.

Peering left out the cockpit, Ostrye saw the two spinning props and wing, and dozens of surrounding bombers amid a backdrop of clouds. B-17s were lanky creatures with slender fuselages and gargantuan wings. They reminded Ostrye of dragonflies. Metallic dragonflies. More than 2,000 B-17s were clustered in box formations enroute to the synthetic oil works at Merseburg.

Merseburg.

Dreaded Merseburg.

It had twice as many anti-aircraft guns as Berlin and some of the most feared Fucking Wolf squadrons in the entire Reich.

The flight from Britain to Merseburg was five hours and they were an hour from IP, the initial point for the bombing run, where Ostrye would normally transfer control of the plane to the bombardier Artipo.

Five hours in the air was a long time under normal circumstances, but this run was an absolute time warp because of the lack of conversation. The crew could talk on the interphone despite the noise and distance separating different sections of the B-17. Usually they would be joking about booze and broads and life before and after the war, but no one felt comfortable talking because of the spooks.

After breakfast and the mission briefing, the *Bachelor's Den* crew had been summoned to the office of Colonel Batson, Commander of the 452nd Bomb Group. The Intelligence Officer Captain Mathis had been present with six men. One looked like an Ivy League quarterback, four others seemed like manicured grunts, and the sixth was a tiny man with chopsticks for arms who reminded Ostrye of a rhesus monkey.

Batson was older but whipcord fit and seemed like he could browbeat a commando half his age. "No M64s today," he said. "These men are your ordnance." Batson pointed at the quarterback. "This is Major Smith. He is in command of the *Bachelor's Den*, not Captain Ostrye. Major Smith will be obeyed unconditionally, no matter how peculiar his orders seem. This mission is classified. Secrecy is paramount. During preflight you will behave as if this is a normal run. You will say nothing to anyone about your cargo. You will not repeat anything you observe on this sortie." Batson glared with severity. "Major Smith has a critical mission which could hasten the end of the war and save thousands of lives. He needs your help to accomplish this mission. This sortie may be the most important thing you ever do. I have informed Major Smith that you are one of our best bomber crews. I have informed him that you are more than up to the task and assured him that your courage will not falter. And I know it will not. Dismissed. And good luck."

When the crew had boarded the *Bachelor's Den*, the six spooks and their strange cameras were already inside. Barely a word had been spoken since.

"Somebody say something," Tucker said. Tucker was TG, the turret gunner. He was isolated in a small spherical turret under the belly of the B-17.

"Powdered eggs giving me the runs," Major Smith said. "Wouldn't feed them to POWs."

"That'd violate the Geneva Convention," Ostrye said.

"Crap out the window," Tucker said. "We're deep enough in Germany you might hit a Nazi."

"Bad luck not to drop some kind of ordnance," the waist gunner Blumenkranz said.

"Spook turd count as collateral damage?" Tucker said.

"He is a powdered egg virgin," Blumenkranz said. "Be a greasy stink bomb."

"An Allied wunderwaffe," Major Smith said. "And I'm not a virgin. Just been a while."

"Wonder what?" Tucker said.

"Wonderweapon," Major Smith said.

"Wonder what the Fucking Wolves would think," Tucker said, "if they saw someone crapping out a bomber window."

"Knowing my luck," Major Smith said, "a Messerschmitt would shoot me in the ass."

They laughed. Ostrye was grateful for it. Spooked crews made mistakes.

"Hey Major Smith, sir," Tucker said. "What we photographing with them huge cameras?"

Smith didn't answer.

"Come on," Tucker said. "We're already sworn to secrecy."

Still no answer.

"That really fast German fighter?" Blumenkranz said. "Loud one that doesn't have a prop?"

"Turbojet powered," the copilot McIntire said.

McIntire sat next to Ostrye in the two-man cockpit. Like everyone on board, he wore a brown sheepskin coat, sheepskin pants, and sheepskin hat, all with white sheep fur linings, and a triangular olive oxygen mask which concealed his nose and mouth. Like all airmen, McIntire also wore his Mae West, a yellow inflatable life vest that resembled a large bib, and his parachute harness. McIntire had straight black hair, boyish good looks, and intelligent brown eyes.

"They say someday all airplanes will be powered by turbojets," the engineer Gassoway said.

"Who's this they?" Tucker said.

"You know," Gassoway said. "Them."

Tucker laughed. "It's all so clear now."

"Mark my words," Gassoway said.

Gassoway was a respected flight engineer and no member of the crew would dispute his pronouncements about aircraft systems. Turbojet engines were so new, a world in which all airplanes utilized them was hard to imagine, but hardly absurd because of their remarkable performance. Allied escort fighters protected bombers from German fighters. The best Allied escort fighter the P-51 Mustang had a maximum speed of about 450 miles per hour, but Kraut turbojet fighters had supposedly been tracked on RDF going more than 600 miles per hour! Pilots told horrifying stories of Kraut turbojet fighters zooming in upon formations of B-17s, downing them, and then flying off so quickly that Mustangs couldn't catch them.

A fighter 150 miles per hour faster than a Mustang! Pondering such lethality made Ostrye's stomach tighten.

Fortunately, Kraut turbojet fighters had only appeared in small numbers, as if being tested, and were not highly maneuverable despite their blazing speed. But every fighter pilot who had fought one said the same thing: if the Krauts produced them in quantity and could improve maneuverability, the air war would become a massacre and the Luftwaffe would be invincible.

Filming Kraut turbojet fighters made sense. Especially if a newer mass-produced version with superior maneuverability had just become operational. Kraut turbojet fighters had first been encountered in the summer of 1944, about six months ago. Had the Krauts performed testing of turbojet fighters, improved the design, and commenced manufacturing?

"Or are we photographing Foo Fighters?" Blumenkranz said.

The mere mention of Foo Fighters caused Ostrye to grip the yoke more tightly. McIntire glanced over, his expression severe. All aircrews in Western Europe knew of the spheres of light that trailed Allied aircraft and stayed with them easily, no matter what evasive maneuvers were attempted. They appeared as translucent, metallic silver spheres in the day, phosphorescent or incandescent balls of fire at night. Usually reddish orange, sometimes other colors, especially green, lightning blue, or white. The spheres were presumed to be a new German weapon. Except they never seemed to attack the planes that sighted them. Rather than comforting crews, this absence of attack tended to unnerve them.

"*Dinah Might* saw Kraut Balls couple days ago over Brunswick," Blumenkranz said. "On her way back from hitting the Volkswagen factory."

"Good girls don't but Dinah might," McIntire said.

"Need more Dinahs," Blumenkranz said. "Less good girls."

"Jake said the Kraut Balls FUBARed their RDF and radio," Tucker said. "Made their engines sputter. Said *Dinah* almost stalled and dropped right out of the sky."

Jake Olson was the waist gunner on *Dinah Might*. He and Tucker had attended basic training together.

"Sergeant Olson," Major Smith said, "will be taught to respect classification."

"Jake only told me."

"Loose lips sink ships," Smith said. "Or down bombers as it were."

"Jake only told me cause we're pals."

"And who are you only going to tell because you're pals? And who are your pals only going to tell because they're pals?"

"No one, sir."

"Sergeant Olson was debriefed after his sighting, ordered not to tell anyone about it, and will be punished for violating that order. As will anyone on this crew who violates secrecy."

Silence returned. And nervousness with it.

2

Major Smith poked his head into the cockpit, gripped the entry-way with a mittened hand, and flipped open his oxygen mask. Straight sandy hair protruded from his shearling cap. Smith had a tanned face, crow's feet and forehead lines, and conscientious eyes.

"Turn off your interphones," he said.

Ostrye and McIntire obeyed and flipped open their oxygen masks. The crew could no longer hear what they said, but they could still hear the crew.

"My presence has impeded morale," Major Smith said to Ostrye. "You should fraternize with your men to rejuvenate their spirits."

"Not leaving the cockpit," Ostrye said.

Smith's eyes seemed to twinkle, and his crow's feet clenched.

"Always by the book," he said. "One of the reasons we chose *Bachelor's Den*."

"Aren't we lucky," McIntire said.

"I'll copilot," Smith said.

"That an order?" Ostrye said.

"It is."

"You a pilot?" Ostrye said.

"I can fly a B-17. Don't know if you want me landing one."

Smith was probably a fighter pilot. B-17s were huge, lumbering aircraft, harder to land than a fighter.

McIntire grabbed his yoke and took control of the plane. The cockpit had dual controls so the copilot could fly if the pilot was killed.

Ostrye waited to be sure McIntire stayed tight in formation and didn't drift towards surrounding aircraft. In box formation, bombers flew in triangular "vee" or echelon formation like migrating birds, and several squadrons in vee were arranged among squares of sky like pieces on a three-dimensional chessboard. *Bachelor's Den* had two other planes in its vee formation, *Dog Breath* and *Cyanide for Hitler*.

Glancing forward and rightward, Ostrye saw *Dog Breath's* left wing, which was set low on the fuselage and angled upward. The massive tail fin was rounded on the top.

Ostrye peered past McIntire out the side window, at *Cyanide for Hitler*. Its wing extended out from the fuselage straight towards Ostrye and almost didn't seem three dimensional. The side profile of *Cyanide for Hitler* seemed devoid of depth, like a shadow.

Bachelor's Den was right where it was supposed to be, left echelon tight off *Dog Breath's* wing and directly left of *Cyanide for Hitler*. Ostrye unhooked his oxygen quick connect, unplugged his suit's heater plug, and unplugged from the interphone. He exited the pilot's seat and waited while Smith situated himself in it.

"Tell your crew not to worry," Smith said.

"Be helpful if that was the truth."

"The first casualty in war," Smith said, "is always the truth."

3

B-17 bombers had ten crew members: a pilot, copilot, bombardier, navigator, radioman, engineer/top gunner, turret gunner, tail gunner, and two waist gunners. Ostrye had eight men to visit, not counting spooks.

Ostrye had been disconnected from oxygen for less than a minute but already felt lightheaded. He plugged his oxygen hose into a supplemental oxygen canister, which he placed in the pocket of his coat. Ostrye stood a moment, sucked some Os, and waited for the lightheadedness to pass.

B-17s had six main compartments. Front to rear, they were the bombardier station in the nose, the cockpit, the bomb bay, the radio compartment, the waist gunner compartment, and the tail. Ostrye was in the cockpit, which was just in front of the wings atop the fuselage. Gassoway stood behind Smith and McIntire manning the top turret, a rotating plexiglass dome from which two fifty-caliber Browning machine guns protruded, one on either side. Ostrye couldn't see the Brownings, but they were there. Gassoway stood on an elevated platform, and the upper portion of his body was pressed up into the turret. He glanced down at Ostrye.

19

Gassoway was almost thirty years old, ancient compared to the rest of the crew, and he looked much older than thirty. His head reminded Ostrye of a boulder, and he had huge bags under his eyes. Ostrye had never seen Gassoway without his baggage, no matter how well rested.

Ostrye nodded at Gassoway, who nodded back with his usual sardonic expression, as if the mission and war and life itself were all some morbid joke whose punchline only he was privy to.

Gassoway never needed coddling. Ostrye kept moving and entered the bomb bay. Bomb racks consumed either side and a nine-inch-wide central plank was the only walkway. Usually, 500-pound M64 gravity bombs would be stacked atop each other in the racks, pullout arming pins in the rear, as if the bombs were gargantuan hand grenades.

Bomb loading crews liked to paint messages on the bombs, and Ostrye usually found at least one message from Sergeant Sandusky that made him laugh. On a run to Berlin a couple weeks back, Sandusky had written "To Hitler with Love" on a colossal 2,000 pound M66. Using lipstick. Inside a red heart with Xs and Os and an actual lipstick kiss.

The absence of his bomb reading ritual discomforted Ostrye. As did the absence of bombs.

A bombless bomber!

Futility personified.

Instead of bombs, six cylindrical, rubberized containers filled the racks, three on each side. Each container was huge, at least the size of an M66, and rounded on the front and square-finned on the rear, just like an M66. A B-17 could never carry six M66s weighing 12,000 pounds, as its maximum load was 4,500 pounds on long runs. This incongruity increased Ostrye's sense of unease. Chalkish white letters stenciled on the containers read: LVAD.

LVAD instead of To Hitler with Love or some other derogation of Krauts.

FUBAR.

So very, very FUBAR.

Ostrye felt a chill, but it had nothing to do with the disheartening absence of bombs or other fears. The cockpit was the warmest region of the *Bachelor's Den*, a balmy thirty below zero, and the interior grew colder as one moved towards the waist gun windows. It was probably forty below zero in the bomb bay. Ostrye's entire body was deadening as the warmth that had been provided by the electrical suit heater was siphoned into the surrounding air. The relentless heat drain was an enveloping sensation, what Ostrye imagined drowning might feel like.

As Ostrye walked the plank towards the radio room, he glanced down at the closed bomb bay doors. He imagined them opening. He would jump out and swan dive. To Hitler with Love would be painted on his chest. He would hit the ground and enter it like water, but instead of a splash there would be an explosion.

Ostrye opened the small door to the radio compartment and entered it. The door was low at the top and did not touch the floor at the bottom, so Ostrye had to duck and step over the floor partition simultaneously. He closed the door behind him. A second door in front of him led to the waist gun compartment. It was closed.

The radioman Strout was sitting at a cramped desk which was pressed into the bomb bay's rear wall on the left side. Radio equipment on shelves lined the walls, thick, heavy-looking metal boxes with dials and meters on the front and wires running in and out the sides. This was the only compartment on *Bachelor's Den* that felt like an actual room inside a building. It was a hell of a long way from comfortable, but still the most bearable place in the bomber.

Strout had Neanderthal features but a scholar's bearing. An evolutionary anomaly. His bushy eyebrows reminded Ostrye of caterpillars.

Extra interphone, heater, and oxygen jacks had been installed in every compartment, for the spooks. Ostrye plugged into the heater and interphone jacks.

"Strange to be on a bomb run with no bombs," Strout said. "Bad omen."

"No need to introduce superstition, Sergeant Strout."

"If you say so, sir."

Ostrye said, "To Hitler with Love."

"That lipstick." Strout chuckled. "Sandusky probably talked a secretary into kissing the bomb."

"And then him."

The crew laughed over their interphones.

"Heard it was Miss Prentice that smooched that M66," Blumenkranz said.

"Lucky bastard," Strout said.

Miss Prentice was Colonel Batson's secretary and the combat wing pinup girl. She was a bombshell with a voluptuous body like Jane Russell's.

Ostrye touched his toes and hung there a moment, praying *Bachelor's Den* didn't hit a pocket of turbulence that would keel him over. It was tough to loosen muscles in the freezing cold. You had to be patient. Ostrye gradually extended his stretch, reaching lower and lower, and then felt his back pop. He sighed with relief and stood.

There were usually two seats across the aisle from Strout where the waist gunners could spell themselves. These had been removed, and a second table and chair had been installed. The chopstick-armed spook that reminded Ostrye of a rhesus monkey sat at the table reading a document. A reading lamp and space heater mounted to the fuselage were both turned on. The rhesus' sheepskin mittens lay on the table but he was still wearing his electrically-heated undergloves. He looked puny in the flight suit, like a child trying on his father's clothes.

Being a pilot, Ostrye had exceptional eyesight and was able to read the document heading: On the Electromagnetic Effects Due to the Motion of Electrification through a Dielectric (1889) by Oliver Heaviside. Whoever Oliver Heaviside was.

The rhesus saw Ostrye snooping, glared, and pulled his papers closer.

"You have a name?" Ostrye said.

"Doctor Devlin," he said without looking up from his reading.

"That your real name?"

"It's what you can call me."

"I've seen you before. In some newspaper photo or something."

"I was occasionally photographed with Nikola Tesla. Prior to his death. More recently, with Doctor Einstein. Upon occasion."

"Heady company."

Devlin kept reading.

"Who was smarter," Ostrye said, "Tesla or Einstein?"

"An impotent question."

"Humor me, oh phallic one."

Devlin's eyes grew smaller yet fiercer, more monkey like. His oxygen mask might have been the semi-spherical lower face of a rhesus.

"Tesla," he said.

"Most people would pick Einstein."

"The simplest way to arrive at truth," Devlin said, "is to determine what most people think and assume the opposite."

"That's not an answer."

"Yes it is."

"I mean an honest answer."

Devlin glared at Ostrye. "What did Einstein ever build?"

He resumed his reading. Ostrye glanced at the document and saw detailed mathematical nomenclature. Not algebra or geometry, which he understood, but intimidating equations with Greek letters, inverted triangles, and copious superscripts and subscripts.

"Was Tesla really insane later in life?" Ostrye said. "Like some newspapers claim?"

Devlin glared again. "You aren't one of those idiots who believes what he reads in newspapers?"

"You're a real charming guy."

"And you ask such insightful questions." Devlin flicked his outstretched hand repeatedly. "Let me read."

Strout and Ostrye exchanged an amused glance. Strout eyed Devlin's space heater with envy and shook his head. Ostrye unplugged from the interphone and heater, patted Strout on the shoulder, opened the aft door, and ducked through the slender entryway, once again stepping above the floor partition. The B-17 fuselage was cylindrical yet decreased in radius as one moved rearward. It was almost 75 feet long, and Ostrye felt as if he was moving through distinct chambers.

Ostrye entered the waist gunner compartment. It was the largest compartment in the bomber, but also the most cramped. Latticework lined the aluminum interior, rising six inches off it. Frozen condensation glistened.

The ball turret was directly in front of Ostrye, protruding through the fuselage floor like a bearing. He saw the top of a silverish aluminum sphere. A quarter of the sphere's height was visible.

Ostrye did the same thing he always did when looking at the ball turret. He shook his head. Only 44" in diameter, the ball turret was remarkably tiny. The smallest crew member was always the turret gunner, and he had it the worst.

The turret was supported by a thick metal A-frame. A bright yellow oxygen canister shaped like a fat pill capsule was mounted longways above the turret on the A-frame. It provided oxygen to Tucker. Many such canisters were situated throughout the fuselage and connected to the oxygen system the crew used to breathe. All oxygen canisters on B-17s were armor plated to mitigate the risk of explosion.

A wide plank walkway was laid over the aluminum latticework. It curved along the left fuselage wall and around the ball turret, and then shot straight down the middle of the fuselage towards the tail gun.

Just past the ball turret, Browning machine guns were mounted waist-high on poles in front of two rectangular windows, one left, one right, staggered because there wasn't enough room in the cramped compartment for gunners to stand back to back. The rounds were almost four inches long and embedded in flexible magazines which hung from the Brownings and entered tall ammunition chests mounted on the walls.

Blumenkranz stood with Monroe, the other waist gunner. Both were blond. Blumenkranz was clean shaven and dimpled. Monroe's stubble and complexion belonged on a cactus.

Ostrye squatted on the plank next to the ball turret and was careful not to hit his head on the oxygen canister. He tapped the turret twice.

"Guns down," he yelled.

Tucker's voice was muffled and difficult to understand.

"You sure?" he said.

The guns were only aimed straight down when the turret gunner was entering or exiting. Any time the ball turret wasn't operational, the underside of the B-17 was defenseless. German fighter pilots knew this. Leaving the guns pointing straight down was a sure way to single out a bomber for attack.

"Positive," Ostrye yelled. "Just for a minute."

"One sec," Tucker said. "Just finishing up my calisthenics."

It was at least sixty below zero in the waist gun compartment. The cold tore at Ostrye. Each breath seemed to flash freeze him from the inside out. Ostrye's lungs felt like a sputtering engine. He knew he wasn't suffocating. It just seemed like it. Ostrye wanted to show his men that he could endure hardship without complaint, so he did his best to maintain a neutral expression.

The turret hydraulics made their pumping sound, motors whirred, and the turret rotated until a hatch became visible. Two small recessions on the hatch contained latch levers. Ostrye flipped them outward, opening the hatch. Tucker pressed upward on the hatch, and it opened.

Tucker was 5'3" and slender but absolutely sardined inside the three foot eight inch wide turret. His feet were planted in heel rests directly below the entry hatch. He was seated and leaning forward until his face was about a foot and a half above his knees and the back of his head rested on the inside of the entry hatch. This allowed Tucker to look through the porthole situated between his feet. Two Browning machine guns on either side of Tucker's body flanked him like pillars. A gun sight and the hydraulic and motor equipment were also inside the turret. Tucker had no room to move. He would be confined in this inquisitor's implement for much of the ten-hour run.

Tucker stood and pressed his torso upward through the open hatch. He wiggled his midsection back and forth, did some neck rolls, flicked his head left and right repeatedly, and grunted with satisfaction when vertebrae presumably popped.

Tucker exhaled deeply. He flipped open his mask, exposing his screwy, endearing grin.

"Hey Cap'n," he said. "How's the field trip going? Major Smith's idea, right?"

Ostrye just smiled.

"No way you'd leave the cockpit," Tucker said. "We all know that. You supposed to bring us some cookies and moo juice? Tell us not to be spooked by the spooks?"

"Something like that."

Tucker laughed.

"You always look so appalled when you peer in here at me Cap'n."

"My subconscious can't accept that a person actually fits in there."

"My aching back and knees have the same problem as your sub-conscious."

"Don't know how you do it," Ostrye said.

"Turret's no place for the claustrophobic," Tucker said. "Can't complain though. Got room for a parachute."

This was more than most of the taller or thicker TGs could say. If forced to join the Caterpillar Club, most were screwed with a four-mile-high S.

Christ, was the ball turret unsafe. Only place on a B-17 more dangerous was in front of the prop.

Tucker shivered and then plugged his flight suit back in. The thermostat was under the turret seat, in a spot he couldn't reach, which was a design flaw. Tucker had no choice but to plug and un-plug his flight suit repeatedly, to roast and then grow cold, roast and then grow cold, roast and then grow cold. Most of the 2,000 turret gunners in surrounding B-17s faced the same torture.

"AAF should recruit a troupe of midgets for turret duty," Tuck-er said.

"You are a midget," Blumenkranz said.

Monroe danced up and down with exaggerated fulcruming of his knees and arms, caricaturing a Munchkin. He spoke in a squeaky voice and said, "Follow the yellow brick road. Tucker's off to see the Fuhrer. Because because because because. He thought that's where his other ball was."

Tucker flicked Monroe off. Monroe continued dancing and be-gan another hackneyed, nonsensical rendition of *Follow the Yellow Brick Road*. Everyone laughed.

"Better get back to my calisthenics," Tucker said. "Close up this sardine tin, would you Cap'n?"

"What you baking after calisthenics?" Ostrye said.

"Croissants," Tucker said. "Lightly buttered."

Tucker breathed in deeply through his nose, as if he could smell them, and then exhaled with contentment.

"Always croissants lately," Ostrye said.

Tucker's expression became positively luminous, but his eyes conveyed longing.

Ostrye stood tall, saluted Tucker, and nodded at him with respect. Tucker smiled his endearing, screwy grin, then closed his mask, reentered the turret, and reassumed the position. Ostrye closed the hatch and flipped the locking levers inward. He then pounded on the hatch twice to let Tucker know it was locked and he was clear. The hydraulics pumped, the motor whirred, and the hatch vanished as the turret spun.

Ostrye closed his mask and walked past the turret towards the waist guns and Blumenkranz & Monroe. Ostrye once again plugged into the extra heater and interphone jacks. Blumenkranz & Monroe seemed impervious to the cold and altitude, as always. Ostrye felt uplifted by their sheer exuberance and indefatigability, as always.

"Put your masks on, B&M," he said to them. "You're hardheaded enough with oxygen."

B&M laughed and obeyed. They squeezed their masks repeatedly, to break off ice buildup on the interior that might clog oxygen intake. As they did so, the balloon-like rebreather bags below their masks jiggled, reminding Ostrye of turkey gobblers.

B&M were the youngest of the crew. Just eighteen. Kids who should have been playing football near some corn field.

Even with a mask on, the angularity of Blumenkranz's face was evident. His eyes were as blue as a mountain lake. Handsome bastard needed a Browning to keep the broads at bay.

"B&M?" Smith said over the interphone.

"Yeah?" they said in unison.

"It was a question," Smith said.

"We like to chase dollies together," Blumenkranz said.

"B&M is like S&M," Ostrye said. "Something torturous you inflict upon broads."

"It's something they love," Blumenkranz said. "Just like S&M."

B&M laughed. There was a palpable thump as they high-fived with their thick mittens, though the engine and wind noise quickly swallowed the sound.

Ostrye shivered. The waist gun windows were open holes in the fuselage which wind rushed in through. It was January. This was the most savage winter Europe had seen in almost a century. It was abominably frigid, even with a shearling shell over an electrically heated flight suit.

"We gotta toughen you up, Captain," Blumenkranz said. "And these spooks."

Two spooks standing near B&M shivered uncontrollably and had despondent expressions, as if marooned with Shackleton. The sheepskin bomber suits looked unnatural on them, like costumes. One rubbed his mittens together incessantly. The other had his arms crossed and was hunched.

"This is insane," one spook with red hair said. His teeth chattered so hard and rhythmically that it was difficult to understand him. "Four and a half miles up with open windows, like it's my front porch in Tucson."

"If there were a p-p-p-polar bear with us," the other spook said, "he'd j-j-j-jump out the window and c-c-c-c-commit suicide."

Blumenkranz rolled his eyes. "Who would have thought spooks would be such pussies?"

"Don't just stand there," Ostrye said to the spooks. "Move around. Only way you'll stay warm."

They obeyed, marching in place and pumping their arms. They clapped their mittens repeatedly, producing hollow thumping sounds that were once again devoured by the engines and wind.

Monroe flipped open his mask, stood near the window, pressed one nostril down with his sheepskin mitten, and blew his nose. A long trail of snot shot out the open nostril, flew out the window, froze instantly, and was whisked away in the slipstream.

"V3 snot rocket!" Monroe said.

Blumenkranz laughed hysterically. The eyes of the spooks dilated with despondence.

Monroe switched nostrils and launched another wunderwaffe. This one also froze instantly, becoming a thin icicle which catapulted end over end and shattered.

The spooks shook their heads.

Blumenkranz laughed even harder.

"Hey spooks?" he said. "Your nuts clinking yet?"

The spooks glanced at each other with expressions of abject horror.

"Only six hours to go," Monroe said.

His laughter was more of a heckle.

Ostrye eyed the two monstrous motion picture cameras mounted on swivels near the Brownings. The lenses were more like telescopes and the film canisters seemed bigger than jeep tires. The cameras were self-encased, as if designed to be concussionproof and waterproof. The shivering spooks stood behind the cameras, ready to photograph on a moment's notice.

"Lot of film," Ostrye said to the red-haired photographer. "Shooting a long time?"

"Short time," the photographer said.

"Then I'm confused."

"This is a Fastax high speed rotating prism camera," the photographer said. "Normal motion picture cameras record eighteen frames per second. This one records five thousand frames per second."

Ostrye whistled. It was a sickly whistle owing to his semi-frozen lips but at least discernable. "How much film is it holding?"

"Reel's got a four-foot diameter. Bell Labs designed a special feed system, so we don't have to place the feed and takeup reels back to back like in a normal camera."

"That was nice of them," Ostrye said.

"Sure was. Otherwise these cameras wouldn't fit inside the fuselage. Least not with enough room to swivel and aim. B-17's maximum internal cross-section is only eight and a half feet."

"Any other bells and whistles?"

"Vibration dampening. Pressurization to prevent condensation on the prisms. Or was it depressurization?" He shrugged. "Something to do with pressure. I'm a photographer, not an engineer."

"You got a fake name?" Ostrye said.

He chuckled. "McGinnon. My partner's Jablonski. Cameras have heaters, too. Keep the film from seizing up or getting ruined by the cold, and once again to prevent condensation. And keep our hands from freezing to them."

"We got the same problem with the Brownings," Blumenkranz said. "Except we don't got no heaters."

"Poor babies," Tucker said. "You're breaking my heart down here. What else you want while they're installing handwarmers for your Brownings? A hotplate and a Joe pot?"

"What's our altitude?" Jablonski said.

"About 23,000 feet," Ostrye said.

"Almost enough film to reach the ground," Jablonski said. "20,000 foot roll, 16 frames per foot, 320,000 frames total. At 5,000 frames per second, that's 64 seconds of filming."

"Only a minute?" Ostrye said.

"A minute," McGinnon said, "is an epoch in high speed photography."

"What you recording that you need a camera so fast?" Monroe said.

"You having sex," Blumenkranz said.

Monroe rolled his eyes. "That seamstress dolly said you ran out of ammo quicker than a Browning."

"Your intel is FUBAR," Blumenkranz said. "That siege lasted longer than Stalingrad."

"And she held out like the Russians."

"Put out, not held out."

"Whatever you say, Aesop."

For once Ostrye didn't find B&M's endless bragging about broads tiresome. Glancing at them and the cameras, he envisioned them as actors on a movie set. Blumenkranz would be the leading man.

"What are high speed cameras usually used for?" Ostrye said.

"To view motion which is too rapid for the human eye to discern," Devlin said. "Obviously."

Ostrye turned and faced Devlin, who was standing just outside the radio compartment on the plank behind the turret.

"I must be dumb," Monroe said. "Cause that wasn't obvious to me at all."

"Many seemingly mysterious phenomenon," Devlin said, "become understandable when viewed in slow motion. High speed cameras were first used to study galloping horses. Prove that all four hooves left the ground. More recently, to observe relay bounce."

"What's relay bounce?" Ostrye said.

"Bouncing of relays," Devlin replied.

"Galloping horses the best you can do?" Monroe said. "Camera like that, you didn't record Babe Ruth hitting a fastball? Or a tornado?"

"Or Jane Russell doing jumping jacks?" Blumenkranz said.

"Pardon our negligence," McGinnon said. "We've only used Fastaxes to record bullets firing and explosions. Things like that."

"Turbojet fighters and Foo Fighters can outperform our planes," Ostrye said, "but they don't move that fast, do they?"

"You wouldn't understand it," Devlin said. "Even if I could tell you."

4

The fuselage narrowed and lowered near the aft, and Ostrye ducked as he approached the tail gunner Kennemer. He saw the soles of Kennemer's boots first and then his back. Kennemer sat upright with his knees forward and his feet tucked under his hindquarter, which was perched on a low stool shaped like a bicycle seat. The seat was the same height as the top of Kennemer's boot soles, angled forward, and kept him from having to be perpetually hyperextended with his hindquarter pressing on his feet. Rectangular pads cushioned Kennemer's shins.

Kennemer's upper body poked up into an enclosed, acrylic windshield mounted behind the B-17's rear fin. Two side-by-side Brownings were below the windshield and in front of his waist. Their muzzles protruded from the tail and were not visible. Kennemer had little room to move and reminded Ostrye of a pet in a travel cage. Only the ball turret was more cramped, and as with Tucker in the ball turret, Ostrye's joints ached envisioning the discomfort that Kennemer endured.

Kennemer was wiping frost off the windshield with his left hand and his right hand was on the handle of his sight. He wore the same three-fingered, shearling mittens as the rest of the crew. They were like lobster claws. Kennemer scanned the sky vigilantly. It was his job to warn of any attacks from the rear. And counter them.

Kennemer's Latin quotes were etched on metal placards mounted on either side of the windshield. There were two identical placards, one on each side. Ostrye read the one on the left.

Bellum omnium in omnes.

A war of all against all.

Urbes constituit aetas, hora dissolvit.

A lifetime builds up cities, a single hour ruins them.

Ostrye didn't speak Latin, and no translations were etched on the placard, but Kennemer had explained the quotes to the crew many times. Except the newest one.

Dulce bellum inexpertis.

Ostrye didn't know what the new quote meant, and though he was curious, he didn't ask. It was unwise to get Kennemer going. They'd made that mistake on an eleven-hour run to the aircraft assembly plant at Resenburg. Kennemer had ranted for the entire sortie.

"Another bright and cheery day in the rear?" Ostrye said.

"Not dead yet," Kennemer said. "But the day's young."

"Could be worse," Ostrye said. "We could be Tail End Charlie."

This was the rearmost and outermost plane on the tail end of a formation, the one most susceptible to fighter attacks.

"Who needs Tail End Charlie," Kennemer said, "when you're carrying spooks."

He finished wiping off the windshield, stood up gingerly, turned around to face Ostrye, and sat back down on the rear portion of the seat as if it were the edge of couch. Kennemer flipped open his oxygen mask and winced as he rubbed his knees. A pretty man with sensitive features, Kennemer had long eyelashes, pouty lips, and sad eyes.

Neither man spoke. Kennemer stared into Ostrye's eyes for almost a minute without saying a word. Ostrye finally rose and said, "Good talking to you."

Kennemer smiled. "The wise man speaks because he has something to say. The fool speaks because he has to say something."

"You're the smartest member of the crew," Ostrye said. "Including me. I'd feel better if you had something to say."

"Not smarter than Doctor Devlin."

"Maybe half as smart." Ostrye unplugged Kennemer's interphone. "But only a quarter the asshole."

Kennemer exploded in laughter. When it subsided he said, "Colonel Batson called the spooks our ordnance. That mean we can drop Doctor Devlin and Major Smith over Merseburg?"

"You can't jettison every asshole you meet in life."

"Why not?" Kennemer said.

"Too many of them."

Ostrye wanted to emphasize the importance of everyone doing their duty and to defend the difficulty of a classified mission he did not fully understand. But Kennemer was too smart for such cheerleading. Or perhaps too jaded. Jaded in a more severe and incurable way than Gassoway.

"Why aren't you an officer?" Ostrye said. "You could have been."

"Don't want responsibility for other people's lives. And I can't stand people."

"Particular people?"

"And the totality," Kennemer said. "Especially the totality."

"Why?"

"Oh come on man."

"I get it," Ostrye said, "but I don't. Humor me. Why?"

"How many heavy bombers has America built?"

"Shit. I don't know."

"About 35,000," Kennemer said.

"I'm no expert," Ostrye said. "But sounds about right."

"It's totally wrong," Kennemer said. "For what it costs to build a heavy bomber like a B-17, you can build a school in thirty cities. Or power plants for 120,000 people. Or two modern hospitals. With the resources wasted just on heavy bombers, America could have built 300,000 schools, 30,000 hospitals, and 20,000 power plants."

Ostrye knew where Kennemer was headed, but interrupting him was difficult. Once Kennemer got going he spat out words faster than a Browning did bullets.

"And that's just the waste in America," Kennemer said. "Then there's the heavy bombers built by our Allies. And the Axis. And medium bombers and light bombers and fighters and transports and tanks and jeeps and rifles and ammo and boots and aircraft carriers and God knows what else. Think of how much we could have educated and healed and nourished people if those resources were used ethically. Used sanely."

"Not our fault," Ostrye said.

"What a copout," Kennemer said. "Whose fault is it then?"

"Hitler's."

"How moronically simplistic."

"Right back at you," Ostrye said. "We're supposed to build schools and hospitals stateside and do nothing while Hitler enslaves the world?"

"With all respect, sir, you can be thick sometimes. Who do you think funded Hitler? We whalloped Germany the first time in the Great War. That was only thirty years ago. We saddle Germany with crushing reparations that caused them to hyperinflate their currency, their whole economy collapses as a result, and less than a decade later they're magically transformed into the largest military power in world history. They had to have help f—"

"Don't abuse the latitude I grant you, Sergeant."

"You ask me to speak freely," Kennemer said. "Then when I say something you don't like, you pull rank. Can't have it both ways."

Kennemer was right. Ostrye paused, deciding what to say or do next. Kennemer exploited the hesitation, and once again expressed his heartfelt view that Wall Street had financed the Nazi industrial juggernaut. He then started ranting about the American-crafted Treaty of Versailles that ended the Great War, arguing that it made the rise of a dictator like Hitler inevitable. Kennemer's vehemence became shrill almost instantaneously. Ostrye had heard it all before many times, and then as now, had no idea how to process it or counter it. He only knew he didn't want to deal with such ludicrousity, especially not in the middle of a run.

Ostrye raised a halting hand.

"Sometimes," he said, "I wonder whose side you're on."

"The side of decency," Kennemer said.

And he began to rant again.

Ostrye raised a halting hand.

"This isn't the time," he said.

"You always say that."

"For once it's true. What you expect me to do? Pull up a chair and shoot the shit for a couple hours?"

"Fair enough," Kennemer said. "But to answer your question, I can't be an officer when I don't believe in war and despise the human race."

Ostrye sighed deeply.

"What in the hell am I going to do with you Kennemer?"

"Leave me alone in the rear."

It occurred to Ostrye that Kennemer would probably always be alone. He said, "Any thoughts on the spook cameras?"

"Anything to change the subject."

"New subject is kind of important," Ostrye said. "Hate for someone who despises war as much as you to die in one."

"You shouldn't overthink a problem."

"Under thinking is my problem," Ostrye said.

"Not mine."

"You can say that again."

Kennemer chuckled. "Maybe the spooks are simply here to photograph a lightning fast new Kraut aircraft. Like it seems."

"Do they really need cameras that fast?"

"Could be simple overkill."

"This whole spook show unnecessary?" Ostrye shook his head. "I doubt that."

"Me too." Kennemer looked up and past Ostrye without focusing on anything. He took an especially deep breath. "There is another possibility."

"Were you going to tell it to me?"

"I can coast down a river slowly in a canoe," Kennemer said, "while flies and mosquitos swarm around me moving much faster than my canoe. So fast they are blurs I can't even see."

"Meaning?"

"Maybe the spooks are here to photograph the mosquitos rather than the canoe."

"What the hell does that mean?"

Kennemer smiled smugly but said nothing.

"Answer me, Sergeant."

Kennemer sprouted a patronizing grin.

"I'm sorry," he said. "This isn't the time."

Kennemer turned around, resituated himself, plugged his interphone back in, and began wiping off the windshield again.

"Sergeant," Ostrye said. "Turn around. That is an order."

Kennemer obeyed. He had a glum expression that reminded Ostrye of a scolded puppy.

Ostrye offered his warmest smile.

"We don't always agree," he said

"We never agree," Kennemer said.

"And we don't have to," Ostrye said. "The fact that we never agree doesn't mean I don't like you. Or hold it against you."

Kennemer sighed deeply.

"I know, sir. It's just." Another deep sigh. "If people don't learn the truth, nothing will ever change. Ten thousand years from now, humans still going to be warring?"

Probably, Ostrye thought.

He said, "We can't change the world today."

Kennemer snorted. "Always tomorrow."

"Today we have to survive. I want you alive tomorrow to change the world."

Kennemer took another extremely deep breath. He held it in several seconds, and then exhaled for several seconds. The anguish in him seemed to subside, though it never went away.

"We're all in this together," Ostrye said. "Don't brood too much back here, okay?"

Kennemer smiled his haunted smile. "Okay, sir. I'll try."

5

Ostrye exited the tail and walked towards the nose of *Bachelor's Den*.
He passed back through the crowded waist-gunner compartment
and the Fastax cameras, moved along the walkway past the ball turret, and entered the radio compartment.

Ostrye turned and peered out the radio compartment door, back
towards the tail. He saw Strout next to him, the turret containing
Tucker, Blumenkranz & Monroe manning the waist guns, and a
portion of the seated figure of Kennemer. It was rare not to be in
the pilot's seat on a mission, and Ostrye was enjoying visiting his
men at their stations. Yet that personal contact also made Ostrye
more cognizant of his sacred responsibility.

Ostrye wasn't just Pilot, but also Airplane Commander, except
when Smith meddled. It was Ostrye's job to keep his men alive. To
do that, Ostrye had to get the most out of them, individually and
collectively. He had to keep them working together, be their coach,
their counselor, their father figure, and sometimes a dictator. This
was a far more challenging task than merely piloting the plane.

If Ostrye failed as a leader, his men would die needlessly and
their families would become amputees. Letters would have to be

written to heartbroken mothers and fathers. Letters full of lies, in which Ostrye duped parents and told them their beloved children had actually died for something.

Ostrye cringed as he conceptualized the thought. Christ was Kennemer corrosive.

Whatever the truth about the war, Ostrye wanted Tucker to live to start his bakery. Wanted B&M to live to sire gaggles of illegitimate children. Wanted Kennemer to live to become a college professor and rage against the world. Wanted Gassoway to live to have some cucumber slices placed on his eyes. Ostrye had come to love his men, foibles and all, and was determined to do right by them.

Usually, choosing right was a straightforward proposition. You did everything by the book, adhering rigidly to procedures designed by experts to minimize risks. In this case, the book had been tossed out and replaced by Major Smith, and it was not at all clear that Smith placed the men first. With an obligation to obey Smith's orders, and a higher responsibility to his men, Ostrye felt conflicted. He hoped to hell Smith didn't force him to choose between mission and men.

Ostrye peered at the waist guns and the huge Fastax cameras mounted next to them. They seemed a physical embodiment of the dichotomy that troubled him. You didn't need an active imagination to picture B&M trying to pivot their Brownings to track Jerrys and bumping into cameras. Four men in the waist gun compartment was too many, even before factoring in the Fastaxes. The waist gun compartment was a giant clusterfuck waiting to happen, and Ostrye prayed it wouldn't cost lives.

6

Ostrye closed the door to the waist gunner compartment. Strout was still seated at the radio table on the left of the compartment, peering out a small, rectanglish window not much larger than his head. He turned away from the window when Ostrye entered, nodded fractionally to acknowledge him, and then cast his glance at Devlin, who was seated at the table on the right side of the compartment and was again engrossed in his reading. Dozens of degrees below zero on a roaring, vibrating bomber, and he sat studying as if in some library. Hard not to admire that kind of dedication, even from an asshole.

As Ostrye plugged back into the interphone he once again eyed the document Devlin was reading. Atop the page was the header: On Vortex Atoms, by Lord Kelvin (Sir William Thomson), 1867.

"What's a vortex atom?" Ostrye said.

"If you are trying to annoy me," Devlin said, "I assure you the tactic is effective."

"Just curious is all. What's a vortex atom?"

"An excellent question," Devlin said. "One which certain physicists are revisiting."

"Because of Foo Fighters and ball lightning?"

Devlin cast a sidelong glance in Ostrye's direction.

"For many reasons," he said.

"Lord Kelvin?" Ostrye said. "Like degrees Kelvin?"

"Someone took a science class."

"I can read and write, too," Ostrye said. "Even multiply."

"Miracles never cease. Since you're such a prodigy, maybe you could learn to stop bothering me."

"I will," Ostrye said. "If you'll tell me what a vortex atom is."

"All praise the Lord Kelvin," Devlin said. "His sermons and epistles always provide revelations."

Devlin's eye's twinkled with amusement.

"Only the one true Lord Kelvin," he said, "can conserve you from entropy."

Ostrye had no idea what Devlin was talking about. He tried to find out, but Devlin ignored him and would say nothing more.

7

Ostrye walked the narrow bomb bay plank and again felt disquieted by the absence of bombs. He ducked through a doorway and entered the cockpit compartment. Brightness shone through Gassoway's top-gun turret, which was at the rear of the compartment. Gassoway was standing between Smith and McIntire and was hunched over slightly so he could see out the front windshield.

Ostrye was accustomed to entering the cockpit and assuming the pilot's seat. It felt odd seeing someone else there. Ostrye's gut response was resentment, which he knew he had no right to feel. He tried to quell it.

Gassoway shuffled a bit to make room for Ostrye. McIntire glanced back at Ostrye. Their eyes locked. There was no worry or warning in McIntire's expression. Which meant Smith knew his business and was at least a competent pilot. Not that Ostrye was going to leave it to chance.

"How's she handling?" he said.

"Like a cement truck with two flat tires," Smith replied. "Everything's normal in other words."

Smith laughed. No one else did.

"So you've flown B-17s before," Ostrye said.

"Figured I'd learn spur of the moment," Smith said. "No time like the present."

"That supposed to be funny?" Ostrye said.

Smith glared at Ostrye. Ostrye glared back.

"Did a bunch of training flights in B-17s," Smith said. "For this mission."

"You could have told us that."

"Yes," Smith said. "I could have."

"That an apology?" Ostrye said.

"I don't owe you an apology."

"What you used to flying?" Ostrye said.

"Not albatrosses like this," Smith said.

"So you're a fighter pilot," McIntire said.

"You done, Captain Ostrye?" Smith said.

"Haven't visited the nose."

"Well let's get to it. Sure you want your seat back."

"My plane back."

"You can have your seat back. After you visit the nose."

"Yes, sir."

8

Directly between and behind the pilot and copilot seats there was a small rectangular hole in the floor. Ostrye entered it feet first. The drop was only a few feet, but there was still that momentary discomforting sensation of dangling into nothingness.

Ostrye felt his feet hit floora firma. He wriggled through the entryway, ducking as he did, and then got down on all fours. He was now in the crawlway underneath the cockpit. The nose compartment was immediately visible and just a few yards in front of Ostrye. Its predominant feature was a clear frontal dome which let in abundant light.

Large batteries had been mounted on either side of the crawlway to power the spooks' monstrous cameras. Additional oxygen canisters were also mounted, to provide the extra oxygen required by the spooks in the nose. Ostrye hoped there were no problems with the spooks' oxygen. Getting to the canisters would be murder.

Ostrye disliked entering the nose compartment. He was not claustrophobic. It was the feeling he could not easily return to his rightful place in the cockpit. Even entering the nose compartment when the plane was on the ground, he still succumbed to this worry.

Ostrye crawled forward perhaps six feet. He was young and healthy, but the combination of cumbersome clothing, crampedness, and cold made him feel rickety. Stabs of pain shot through his knees.

Ostrye squeezed through a squat entryway and stood. The brightness was more overpowering. It almost assaulted him. Yet it also beguiled him, drawing him forward. Ostrye pressed his way past the men and equipment crammed in the nose compartment, barely noticing them, and stood in the absolute front of the B-17.

The nose of the aircraft was fitted with a clear acrylic dome that provided a panoramic view. Wisps of cloud frolicked past the nose and a plush mass of clouds filled the sky below the B-17 squadrons. They gave the illusory sense that you could leap into them and have your fall arrested.

Ostrye was able to look straight down out the dome, as if standing on the edge of a skyscraper's roof. He was immune to vertigo or he would have washed out in pilot training, and found the sensation exhilarating rather than frightening. Ostrye felt like a bird gliding through the air.

This was a far better view than the one from the cockpit, which always made Ostrye envious. Not that he disagreed with the methodology. If the bombardier could not obtain a clear view of the target and hit it, the entire sortie was a waste of time. When the bomber was actually carrying bombs anyway.

The renowned Norden bombsight was right next to Ostrye, centered directly in front of the nosedome. A small console with a downward pointing eyepiece atop it, the Norden looked like a cross between a camera and a shop tool.

A chair was behind the Norden and the bombardier Artipo sat in it. Artipo opened his mask and flexed it to remove ice buildup, revealing fish lips and a schnozzle that could smell the soup from five miles out. When Artipo closed his mask his wide eye sockets predominated. Calculating eyes filled them.

Four more Fastax cameras encircled the Norden and two photographers manned them, standing ready to film. One photographer was chubby, with piggish pink cheeks and a fleshy face that bulged up around his mask like a gasket. The other photographer had an elongated face, reddish-brown skin, and might have been Mayan.

The astrodome was normally the only spacious part of the plane and was typically roomy enough for a tea setting. With four cameras crammed in, it was an epic clusterfuck, even more so than the waist gun compartment, which was probably why Lieutenant Artipo seemed so miffed.

"Deputy Lead Able Squadron with all these spooks playing Hitchcock?" He shook his head. "Fucked Up Beyond All Recognition. My CEP will be half a mile."

CEP stood for circular error probable. It was a circle drawn from the exact center of target, which half of bombs fell within. The more accurate the bombardier, the smaller the CEP. With a smaller CEP, more bombs hit the target and inflicted greater damage.

The navigator Forrest sat at a small rectangular table pressed into the left fuselage wall behind the bombardier station. *Bachelor's Den* crew members called each other by their last names. Except for Forrest Hanlon, who was gangly, with a thick crop of curls like a tree canopy. The navigator had to find the metaphorical trees in the forest, which also made Hanlon's first name more apt to the crew.

"I could gouge your eyes out," Forrest said to Artipo, "and your CEP would still be less than two hundred yards."

"Artipo won't be happy till the CEP is ten feet," Monroe said. "Even if we all die."

Artipo was one of the best bombardiers in the Eighth Air Force and was pathological about accuracy. On several previous runs, he had made the formation circle back to the target, giving Kraut fighters a chance to regroup and down additional B-17s.

Artipo glared at the Fastax cameras with irritation.

"If things go badly and we're forced to take lead," he said, "I might not be able to drop the M64s in a pickle barrel."

Bombers flew in tightly-clustered box formations to maximize bombing accuracy. All bombers did not aim independently. Rather, the lead bomber in each box formation determined when to drop its bombs and all other planes followed suit. If the lead bomber aimed accurately and all bombers were formed tightly around it, bombs hit their target.

On this run, there were 40 box formations of 54 bombers each, which was 2,160 bombers, plus 960 fighter escorts. 22,560 men were risking their lives to drop bombs aimed by 40 lead bombardiers.

There were nine M64s per bomber, more than 19,000 bombs. At 274 pounds of explosives per M64, this was 2,603 tons of TNT. In less than an hour, more than 5 million pounds of destruction would rain down upon Germany and decimate its petroleum production—if the aim of the 40 lead bombardiers was true. If not, the entire ordeal was for naut.

It was critical to have the best bombardiers in lead planes. The squadron of lead planes was designated Able Squadron. German fighter pilots knew this and attacked lead planes with suicidal abandon. Except for Tail End Charlie, lead was the most dangerous place to be. And where *Bachelor's Den* now was.

By convention, the bomber right echelon behind the lead took its place if it was downed. *Cyanide for Hitler* was right echelon behind the lead *Dog Breath*. If *Dog Breath* and *Cyanide for Hitler* were both downed, *Bachelor's Den* would take lead and aim the bombs for the entire box formation. *Dog Breath* was Lead of Able Squadron, and *Cyanide for Hitler* and *Bachelor's Den* were Deputy Leads.

Early in the war when the Luftwaffe, the German Air Force, was still fearsome and few bombing runs had fighter escorts, half of the bombers on a run were often downed. But the Luftwaffe had been decimated and Allied air superiority was nearly absolute. Small bombing runs were rarely attacked anymore, and large runs encountered only token fighter resistance—except at a few heavily-fortified positions like Berlin, Misburg, and Merseburg. Earlier in the war Deputy Leads would often have to assume Lead, and though less frequent now, it was still not uncommon.

"You can't drop M64s in a pickle barrel," Forrest said to Artipo, "when we don't have any M64s."

"Shit," Artipo said. "I keep forgetting we don't have bombs."

"We all keep forgetting," Blumenkranz said.

"Easy to take it for granted," Forrest said, "that a bomber will be carrying bombs."

"What's next?" Gassoway said. "A fighter that won't fight?"

"This is so FUBAR," Artipo said. "Why would they make us Deputy Lead if it's impossible for us to lead the run?"

"Why can't we lead the run?" the chubby photographer said.

"When other bombers see the lead bomber drop its bombs," Artipo said, "they drop their bombs. It's a signal. If we don't have bombs, we can't signal. We can't take lead, which means we shouldn't be in Able Squadron."

"You can't send a message to drop bombs by radio?"

"You can," Artipo said, "But radio isn't reliable. Radio signals can get FUBARed. Radio comm also creates a delay that harms bombing accuracy. Plummeting bombs are a simple and emphatic signal that can't be mistaken. And believe me, when the flak starts flying, everything that can go wrong will. You want simple. Simple and reliable."

Major Smith entered. He moved in the sheepskin flight suit naturally, as if used to it.

"Jesus," he said. "I'd forgotten how loud these Flying Fortresses are."

"My sister wanted to know what the engines sound like," Artipo said. "Told her to stand at the base of Niagara Falls for ten hours."

They laughed.

"Please turn your interphones off again," Smith said.

They obeyed.

"I'd prefer two pilots in the cockpit," Ostrye said.

"This is important," Smith said.

"So's having a copilot to fly the plane if the pilot is incapacitated."

"I'll be quick," Smith said. "If *Dog Breath* and *Cyanide for Hitler* are downed you will claim to have a malfunction and let *Borrowed Time* or *Tangerine* take lead. But you will not relinquish your left echelon Deputy Lead position. Not under any circumstances. Is that clearly understood?"

Everyone understood.

Except they didn't.

9

Ostrye was finally back where he belonged, in the cockpit piloting the plane. He let the crew settle back into their routines and then had McIntire turn off his interphone mic. Ostrye did the same. They could hear the crew in case anyone had problems, but the crew couldn't hear them.

"Why you think the spooks are here?" Ostrye said. "Foo Fighters?"

McIntire shrugged. "Beats me."

"So many stories about Foo Fighters," Ostrye said. "Tough to know what's bunk and what isn't."

"If you told me you saw a Foo Fighter," McIntire said, "I'd believe you."

"You trust everyone," Ostrye said. "That's your problem."

"Too many pilots and crews have reported Foo Fighters. They have to be real."

"I don't know," Ostrye said. "How many times have we misidentified something? Or seen some glint or glow or trick of light we couldn't explain?"

McIntire peered out the cockpit window as if trying to identify something and nodded absently. Stare at the sky long enough and your mind would play tricks on you. This happened to every pilot eventually.

Humans weren't birds. They had evolved on the ground hunting mammals, not Messerschmitts. Humans processed reality using multiple senses. Encased in a cockpit with roaring engines, sight became predominant and other senses were neutered. Dislocation resulted. Unable to reconcile the visual sense using other senses, the mind struggled to interpret what it saw and often erred.

Pilots spent hours scrutinizing acres of sky for one blip that might be the enemy aircraft which killed them. Such intense mental focus pulverized the psyche. Add in cold, fatigue, the stress of combat, and maybe even a hangover, and a pilot could get loopy and see things that weren't there. This wasn't insanity or even instability, merely sensory overload.

What had you seen?

Sometimes it was impossible to be sure, and this had been true long before Foo Fighters were first sighted in 1940.

"You'd believe me if I told you I'd seen a Foo Fighter," Ostrye said to McIntire. "And I'd believe you. But the cold hard truth is that there are a lot of crappy pilots. Men that are fundamentally weak. Guys with cognacitus seeing tits in every cloud. Others beginning to crack, destined for Section Eight."

"I can accept that many Foo Fighter sightings are misidentifications, nutters, or errant meteorological phenomenon," McIntire said. "Maybe St. Elmo's Fire or ball lightning, like the barstool experts argue. But we live or die by our ability to identify threats rapidly and accurately. You'll never get me to believe that every single one of the hundreds of reported sightings is erroneous or unreliable."

Silence.

Ostrye might not agree, but he wasn't disagreeing.

"Remember Lieutenant Schlueter," McIntire said.

Ostrye nodded. "From Oshkosh."

They'd met him in a pub, on leave. After a few brewskies, he'd told them about his Foo Fighter encounter. Bright balls of light had ghosted him, responded evasively, and acted with seeming intelligence. Schlueter was a decorated pilot who flew night patrols in P-61 Black Widows, which was as dangerous as it got.

"Schlueter wouldn't last a week if he couldn't identify threats competently," McIntire said. "You're telling me a pilot that good can't tell the difference between St. Elmo's Fire and a Jerry?"

McIntire shook his head.

"No way," he said. "No way a pilot that good makes a mistake that galling."

"Even the best pilots aren't infallible."

"So you don't believe Schlueter?" McIntire said.

"I didn't say that."

McIntire was probably right. The credible cases might be outnumbered by the dubious ones, but there were still a lot of topnotch pilots like Schlueter who were emphatic that the Foo Fighters they encountered were aircraft.

"You assume," Ostrye said, "that what we hear about Foo Fighters is the truth."

McIntire stopped scanning the sky, glanced at Ostrye. "Why would crews lie?"

"Smith threatened us and the waist gunner Olson from *Dinah Might*. How many crews that saw Foo Fighters have been debriefed, intimidated by spooks, told to omit a few key details, maybe fabricate some?"

McIntire resumed his scan of the sky. "Like in the newspapers," he said.

"Yeah," Ostrye said. "Modestly successful run, *Stars and Stripes* and the *New York Times* make it sound like we blockbustered a hole straight to hell and took out the devil."

"Artipo could probably hit the devil right between the horns."

"Yeah," Ostrye said. "He's a sniper, not a bombardier. And what about friendly fire? Or two bombers who accidentally hit each other and go down? That run to Zeitz, lost more than fifty Fortresses but didn't put a single bomb on target? Or the Schweinfurt run. Five ball bearing factories in a neat row west of town, we didn't hit one and lost sixty Fortresses. Ever seen an article about FUBARs like that in *Stars and Stripes* or the *Times*?"

"Never."

"Censorship does that with mundane bomb runs," Ostrye said, "how you think they distort the perception of some highly classified Nazi weapon?"

Ostrye glanced out the small window above him, saw sky and clouds and the bellies of nearby bombers. Also the smaller, more distant P-51 fighter escorts, whose undersides were sleeker, and which had a single front prop rather than two on each wing like B-17s. Fighter escorts sure were a comforting sight!

Ostrye peered back out the front windshield, which seemed simultaneously huge and tiny. The windows were as big as it was possible to make them and allowed a view of much of the sky, yet much of the cockpit was unwindowed, a blindspot. Ostrye longed for a cockpit like the nosedome, one which allowed an unmolested frontal view. Yet even then he would still probably feel unsafe, worry about attacks from behind and from the side, and long for some other more omniscient view system with no blind spots. It was what he couldn't see that worried Ostrye. He envisioned Foo Fighters as clear plexiglass spheres whose pilots could see everything around them. Ostrye knew this was fanciful, but it was what he envisioned.

"So what are the Kraut Balls?" McIntire said. "A new German weapon?"

"That doesn't attack anything?"

"A mission profile we can't discern?" McIntire said.

"Or a known mission profile crews are being forced to lie about."

"Kind of figured Kraut Balls were some experimental craft being prepared for operational use," McIntire said. "Lots of sightings, but never more than a dozen or so seen at once. Maybe there's only a few dozen Kraut Balls. Maybe the Germans are testing their performance and will build a newer Kraut Ball. One that will attack."

"That creepy rhesus monkey looking nerd," Ostrye said, "is probably a genius."

"Rhesus monkey?" McIntire laughed. "Probably not as smart as he acts, or they wouldn't risk him on a suicide run to Merseburg. Think they'd do that with Einstein?"

Ostrye remembered Devlin's haughty words. What did Einstein ever build?

"Suppose the rhesus monkey is as smart and important as he acts," Ostrye said. "We don't have many geniuses. What threat could worry the Brass so much that they'd sacrifice one?"

McIntire had no answer.

10

The worst part of a bombing run wasn't the attack by Nazi fighters, it was the anticipation of that attack and the relentless stress of remaining ready for it. It was not easy to remain vigilant for hours on end, petrified that the five seconds you took to piss or pick your nose or stare absently into space dreaming about some dolly might be the one time a fighter attacked, the single lapse that cost you and your entire crew their lives.

Stress borne of fear descended upon *Bachelor's Den*, enveloped it like a cocoon, and gradually increased in intensity, becoming something palpable the crew could feel as surely as the cold, noise, or vibration.

Someone began humming into their interphone. The rest of the crew joined in. They hummed the *Colonel Bogey March* in unison.

"Dah-dum," the crew hummed, "dah-dah-dah deet-deet dummm."

"Dah-dum," they paused, "dah-dah-dah deet-deet dummm."

"Dah-dum," another pause, "dah-dah-dah dee-dum."

"Da-da-da dee-dum," another pause, "dah de-dum, dah daaahhh."

The virtue of a march was its simplicity. It gave you something else to concentrate on without destroying your focus. The crew was less petrified as they scanned the skies, Artipo and Forrest in the nose, Ostrye and McIntire in the cockpit, Gassoway on the top turret, Tucker in the ball turret, Blumenkranz & Monroe on the waist guns, and Kennemer in the rear. They hummed the *Colonel Bogey March* again, and again, and again. Soon even the photographers joined in.

The crew began singing to the rhythm.

"Hitler, has only got one ball."

"Goring, has two but very small."

"Himmler, is somewhat sim'lar."

"But old Goebbels, has no balls, at all!"

The crew whistled the rhythm several times, and then sang again. They sang several times, and each rendition grew a little bawdier, more cheerful.

Amid the backdrop of song, the engines still roared and vibrated the plane as if trying to shake it apart. The cold still crept through the bomber, pilfering precious heat. And the *Bachelor's Den* and its unfortunate crew still pressed inexorably northeastward, towards the single most fortified bombing target in all of Nazi Germany.

11

"Something seems to be closing in," Blumenkranz said.

Ostrye scrutinized the sky to his left. Something shiny reflected sunlight in the distance. As it drew closer, sunlight danced from multiple points. Several objects rather than one?

"Why haven't our fighter escorts engaged?" Blumenkranz said.

"Start filming." Smith spoke rapidly but calmly. "Two cameras only. One nose, one waist gun. No one is to open fire."

"What the hell is that?" Tucker said.

Numerous silver blips became visible. About the size of a dime held at arm's length, they were still far off but closing quickly.

"Why are the Mustangs beating their meat?" Blumenkranz said.

With startling rapidity, the silver blips accelerated towards *Bachelor's Den*. They became blurs reminiscent of shooting stars. The blurs decelerated abruptly and became silver spheres. The sheer speed of their approach was disorienting. They didn't lurch as any conventional aircraft or other moving object would when decelerating, but rather came to a complete stop instantaneously. Their motion was perfectly controlled and smooth.

Ostrye's stomach tensed, his pulsed quickened, and his throat seemed suddenly dry.

They were dead.

Some German operator on the ground or in a nearby observation plane was going to press a button and detonate the Kraut Balls remotely. That or a proximity fuse would engage. Except there had never been a report of Foo Fighters detonating or attacking. And if detonation had been the intent, the Foo Fighters would have spread out amongst numerous bombers, not stayed in a group, and might have rammed *Bachelor's Den* to maximize explosive damage.

"I say again," Smith said. "No one is to open fire."

Ostrye calmed. Seven spheres hung in the air like balloons yet were moving 182 miles per hour along the same bearing as the B-17, about twenty feet off its left wing. The spheres stretched out parallel to the plane's fuselage. The closest sphere was directly off the wing tip, with three spheres on either side, fanned back to form a gradual vee formation more like a mildly curved line.

Ostrye didn't like having anything so close his wing. Not a friendly, and certainly not Foo Fighters. Turbulence could easily jostle a bomber, causing it to drift ten or twenty feet. Ostrye now had to be even more vigilant, ready to respond instantly if *Bachelor's Den* drifted and prevent it from smashing into the Foo Fighters. He was taut in his seat, adrenaline coursing through him.

The spheres were all the same size and looked to be two to five feet in diameter. The separation between each sphere was three to four times the width of any single sphere. This felt sloppy and amateurish to Ostrye. In tight formation, B-17s were supposed to maintain separation equal to about one wing length or about half their width.

The spheres produced no exhaust and had no prop, turbojet engine, or rocket engine. Nothing which could reasonably be interpreted as a form of propulsion. Except perhaps the translucent sheath that seemed to encase each sphere, which blurred each one, and which seemed to be deformed fractionally by the onrushing wind.

Could the translucent sheath be the propulsion?

It had to be.

What else could be?

But how did it propel the sphere?

If it even propelled the sphere.

And either way, what was it?

Ostrye peered at the spheres, squinted, and tried to discern something in the metallic brightness that would give a clue about the propulsion method. It was futile. The spheres were too blurry. And too shiny, reflecting too much sunlight.

Ostrye tore his gaze from the spheres and glanced over at McIntire. McIntire's brow was furrowed and he glared back ominously.

"Those high speed cameras," he said, "are beginning to make a little more sense."

12

In the bombardier station, the Mayan-looking photographer Rodriguez was hunched, right eye pressed into the camera's eyepiece, right mitten holding the lever which swiveled on its support stand, left mitten gripping the lens at the front. The recording camera sounded like a deck of cards being shuffled rapidly.

The Fastax was turned left, filming not out of the spacious nosedome, but rather a window just behind it on the left side of the fuselage. Rodriguez gritted his teeth as he struggled to photograph all seven of the glowing orbs. He wanted to pan and zoom to get a better shot of the hovering oddities, but the window did not allow this. Probably better to keep it simple with a high-speed camera anyway.

Had the Foo Fighters raced up from the front of the B-17, the shot would have been easiest, as this was the direction the acrylic nosedome faced. The next best vantage would have been out the side of the nosedome, but the camera was not situated far enough forward to allow this. The photographers had foreseen this problem when supervising the mounting of the cameras, and suggested removing the Norden, but the military balked. A B-17 without a Norden in the nose would be too conspicuous. Crews on the ground and in the air would notice. Unfortunately, with the Norden front and center you couldn't mount the cameras forward far enough for rear-facing side shots out the nosedome.

So here Rodriguez was, shooting what was probably the most important film in U.S. military history out a small window with limited vantage. At least the window was acrylic and not just an open hole, so Rodriguez didn't have to freeze his ass off even more, like those poor bastards in the waist gun compartment.

The orbs were eerie bastards. They seemed like metallic fireflies, except they didn't zip around like fireflies. They also reminded Rodriguez of globules of mercury. He didn't know what the orbs were and had heard enough on the interphone to know he was better off not knowing. More importantly, he had seen enough to know he was better off not knowing. If you had a brain, you only had to glimpse the orbs for an instant to realize they were aircraft and the military was going to control them at any cost, killing anyone that got in the way.

Some people couldn't compartmentalize their curiosity. Rodriguez had never had this problem. And he had never been more thankful for that fact than in this moment. When *Bachelor's Den* landed—if it landed—security was going to drop like an M66 and the crew was in for the rudest of awakenings. It wasn't going to go well for them, Rodriguez suspected. Not well at all.

If Rodriguez didn't utter another syllable the rest of the flight, that was fine by him. It would simplify the debriefing, and who knew, maybe they'd even let him live. Looking at the Foo Fighters though, he rather doubted it.

Smith was hunched in behind Rodriguez, breathing down his neck and peering out the window.

Smith.

Rodriguez snickered inside his mask.

Smith was a Yale prick with all the right connections. You probably had to go back ten generations to find someone in his family who'd gotten their fingernails dirty. Smith had deferred his trust-funded education to become a flyboy. A friend of Rodriguez's who was usually right about such things said that Smith had been personally chosen for this command by Wild Bill Donovan and Allen Dulles. If those two names didn't scare you, you were too dumb to live long. The goldenboy of ruthless, OSS bastards like Dulles and Donovan would probably garrote you for a nickel. Smith wasn't to be trifled with. Or trusted.

"You film them accelerating towards us?" Smith asked.

"Got 'em," Rodriguez said. "Don't know how clear they are, but I got 'em."

Smith formed his hand into a fist and pumped his arm back and forth several times quickly.

Rodriguez continued to film the eerie silver orbs. They were twinkling almost like stars in the camera, looking bluish rather than silverish. Was this a trick of the light or lens, or a genuine change? The effect came and went and was difficult to gauge.

"Seen some strange things," Forrest said. "But this takes the cake."

Artipo nodded. "Like the Artful Dodger at a wedding."

"Hey Rodriguez," Forrest said. "You seeing anything we're not?"

Rodriguez shrugged.

And kept his mouth shut.

13

Smith exited the nose, scurried through the crawlway, leaped up into the cockpit, and raced towards the waist gunner compartment. As he moved past the radioman Strout he opened his mask and said, "Inform me of radio disturbances, no matter how minute."

"Informed," Strout said. "Interference ever since those Foo Fighters rolled up. Exactly the sorts of malfunctions we experience when we a—"

"Are in a lightning storm," Smith said.

"Right," Strout said. "Except much mo—"

"More severe," Smith said.

Smith entered the waist gunner compartment while closing his mask. He saw B&M, Doctor Devlin, McGinnon, and Jablonski assembled near the left window. All seemed stunned except Doctor Devlin. McGinnon's eye was pressed into the camera, and he was filming. Smith plugged into the interphone.

"How in the hell can they move so fast?" Blumenkranz said. "And stop so fast? And just hover like that?"

"You filmed them accelerating?" Smith said to McGinnon.

"Looked like they teleported," McGinnon said. "But yeah."

"Won't look like they teleported at 5,000 frames per second," Smith said.

"Better not," McGinnon said. "Wouldn't want you and Doctor Devlin any more paranoid."

"How clear will the images be?"

"Ain't a miracle worker," McGinnon said. "All this plane vibration, only a split second to adjust the lens focus, not making any guarantees."

"Best guess?"

"It'll be in focus for a portion of the trajectory but not all of it. Since it was coming towards us, the focal length was changing. Camera and object this fast, impossible to adjust the focus on the fly."

The Foo Fighters continued to hover off the wing, like ornaments hanging from a tree.

"Might have been easier if the Foo Fighters had been moving parallel to us rather than towards us," McGinnon said. "Focal length would have varied less. Except then I would have had to try and swivel the camera to follow an object that blazing fast. Damn near impossible. At least with them racing towards us they remained in view the entire time."

"Love to have x-ray vision like Superman's right now," Blumenkranz said. "Look right inside that Kraut Ball and see how it flies."

"If only it were that simple," Devlin said.

"Best we might have hoped for," McGinnon said, "is have it run semi-parallel to us from a ways away. Then it would have moved through our field of vision more slowly, and I might have been able to swivel fast enough to record it. Maybe. Except farther away it is, less detailed the images are. And they move so damn fast good chance I would have missed the shot entirely."

"Flash Gordon," Jablonski said, "might've missed that shot."

"You know how they fly," Monroe said to Doctor Devlin. "Don't you?"

Devlin ignored him.

"Things we film usually have fixed focal length," McGinnon said. "We set up a camera in front of a gun or bomb, focus it, fire or detonate at a predetermined time. Easy to get a good shot. Bit harder to sit in a bomber like a nature photographer in debilitating cold and use a five foot tall high speed camera to record an object that appears randomly and follows an unknown and erratic trajectory." McGinnon chuckled and shook his head. "Even my friends in Hollywood wouldn't believe this."

"But you were skilled enough to get the shot," Smith said.

"Lucky enough," McGinnon said.

"Bit of both."

"Mostly luck."

"We'll take it," Smith said.

"Could you give me one little hint?" Monroe said to Devlin. "Just to make it sporting?"

Monroe conveyed earnestness and humility. Devlin smiled. His eyes softened.

"It's simple," he said. "So simple it would scare you."

"Will I find out after the war?"

"Not if we do our jobs right," Smith said. "But the simplest secrets are often the hardest to keep. Now stow the questions."

"Not knowing something so cool is maddening," Monroe said.

The camera's shuffling deck sound softened.

"Almost cooked this reel," McGinnon said.

A few seconds later, the camera made a rhythmic flapping sound. McGinnon shut it off, stood, and peered out at the hovering, translucent orbs which seemed to keep pace with the bombers effortlessly. His smile was wistful.

"Once in a lifetime shot," he said, "and I'll never be able to tell anyone about it."

14

The left camera in the waist-gun compartment was expended. The cameras could not be reloaded and the Foo Fighters continued to hover off the left wing, so Smith had McGinnon and Jablonski move the expended camera into the radio compartment and plug it into a heater. The right waist-gun camera was moved to the left side. McGinnon and Jablonski were so excited to have gotten the shots of the Foo Fighters that they barely noticed the cold. Or stopped complaining about it at least.

The Kraut Balls were still about twenty feet off the *Bachelor's Den* wing, amid the box of bombers. A squadron of bombers was above and behind *Bachelor's Den* on the left. A squadron was also below and behind *Bachelor's Den* on the right. As *Bachelor's Den* was the leftmost plane in the lead squadron, its front and right were directly obstructed by *Dog Breath* and *Cyanide for Hitler*, but there was plenty of open sky from the eight o'clock to eleven o'clock positions, especially low, below the aircraft. This was where the Foo Fighters had zipped in from.

Yet the fact that there was a space in the sky that allowed the Foo Fighters to approach did not mean there was a hole in the formation in terms of defenses. Bombers in Baker Squadron, the squadron above and left of Able Squadron and *Bachelor's Den*, should have opened fire on the Foo Fighters. Except the Foo Fighters had moved too fast to track. Once visible, they were dangerously close to the wing of *Bachelor's Den*.

Hanging tight on the wing was smart.

Damn smart.

It made it impossible for surrounding gunners in other bombers to fire at the Foo Fighters out of fear of accidentally downing *Bachelor's Den*. This negated the primary advantage of the box formation, focusing firepower from multiple Fortresses against enemies.

It was also risky for a bomber to shoot an aircraft extremely close to it, especially if that aircraft wasn't on an attack vector that would carry it away from the bomber once damaged, as was usually the case with attacking fighters. The aircraft might explode and heave shrapnel and parts, damaging or downing the bomber. The Foo Fighters were certainly close enough to *Bachelor's Den* to be a serious risk in this regard.

The more Blumenkranz thought it through, the more impressed he became.

Those Kraut bastards.

Those clever Kraut bastards.

So other bombers couldn't engage the Kraut Balls, and *Bachelor's Den* might not even be able to. But what about the fighter escorts? Even if they were having takeout delivered when the Foo Fighters first approached, they should have engaged by now. Multiple bomber pilots could have radioed the Mustangs, and at least one bomber should have radioed. Mustangs weren't called Mustangs for no reason. They could gallop in and close quicker than you could buzz a whisker. And should have.

But hadn't.

Standing in the waist gun window, looking directly at the Kraut Balls without even a pane of glass impeding his view, Blumenkranz couldn't figure it out. Was there a Major Smith on every bomber in the formation? There sure couldn't be one on every Mustang. They were one-seat fighters. Had 3,120 planes been ordered not to engage the Foo Fighters or speak about them over radio? Nothing had been mentioned in the mission briefing that Blumenkranz had attended with other crews, and such an action didn't jibe with the secrecy Batson had said was so important. Bombers had standing orders not to approach Foo Fighters, however, and an additional order not to shoot at them wasn't highly suspicious, especially not on a single mission. You experienced so many senseless and unexplainable things in war it was impossible to categorize or comprehend them all, and you could go crazy trying.

Who knew what the hell was actually going on?

Major Smith? Doctor Devlin? The people who gave Smith and Devlin orders, whoever they were?

It was all far above Blumenkranz's pay grade. That was all he knew for sure.

But he hated the idea of standing there staring at Foo Fighters and not engaging them. He was a gunner. He existed solely to down enemy aircraft. And here sat seven Jerrys ghosting them so close and nonevasively he could hit them with a slingshot. This was a gunner's wet dream! Yet he couldn't fire. Damn it was frustrating!

Blumenkranz was thus pleased when Major Smith approached and said, "What you think about shooting a Foo Fighter?"

"You afraid of damaging the wing or engines?" Blumenkranz said.

"Not afraid. Aware of the risk though."

"Fuel tanks are in the wings."

"I know."

"I think I'm a gunner," Blumenkranz said. "I'd rather die shooting than standing here with my fist up my ass."

Smith laughed heartily. "Well spoken, Sergeant. Couldn't have said it better myself."

"I don't think shooting at the Foo Fighters is a good idea," Ostrye said. "Shrapnel could easily enter number one and number two engines and damage the wing to t—"

"I wasn't asking what you thought," Smith said.

"I'm the pilot," Ostrye said. "Maybe you should be asking me."

"Well I'm not," Smith said.

"Sorry, Captain Ostrye," Blumenkranz said.

"Doctor Devlin," Smith said. "What is your assessment?"

Doctor Devlin was standing next to Smith, peering at the Foo Fighters intently. His neck cricked outward from the front of his body, as if he were a turtle and his shearling were his shell. Devlin was so short, tiny, and quiet that he was easy to overlook.

"The rotational kinetic energy released," Devlin said, "could be substantial. But I don't see that we have a choice. We knew the risks when we volunteered."

"Did you say rotational?" Kennemer said.

"We didn't know the risks," Gassoway said. "And we didn't volunteer."

"Shoot one of the wunderwaffe," Smith said to Blumenkranz. "And take care not to hit one in front of wing. Or a friendly."

Blumenkranz grabbed the M2 handles. They were close together at the rear of the weapon, vertical, and much larger than his hands. It felt good to grab them. To finally be doing what he was trained for.

Blumenkranz sized up the Kraut Balls judiciously, with a marksman's eye. The effective range of the Browning M2 machine gun was 2,000 yards. That was the claim Browning made in the manuals anyway. Maybe it had that range on the ground for infantry, but in the air if you wanted to actually hit anything you had to limit yourself to about a quarter of that. Fortunately, the Kraut Balls were within fifty yards. Without wind, Blumenkranz could probably have hit one with his pistol.

"You ready, Sergeant?" Smith said.

"Goddamn right I am, sir!" Blumenkranz said. "Fuckers get any closer they'll be able to hop up on the wing and go for a ride. Let's take 'em out!"

"I wonder," Smith said, "if Captain Ostrye could keep a Kraut Ball balanced on the wing."

"Maybe I should practice on you first," Ostrye said.

"I might accept that offer," Smith said. "From a better pilot."

"Ready when you are, sir," Blumenkranz said.

"Don't shoot until we begin filming," Smith said.

"If the Kraut Balls were hostile," Kennemer said, "wouldn't they have rammed us or shot us down before we could react?"

"They are German," Smith said, "and they are hostile. And spare us your pussified pacifism. Unless you wanna preach it from a brig."

Blumenkranz aimed his Browning at the Kraut Balls. Then he tensed and steeled himself, as if expecting the Kraut Balls to fire back.

They didn't.

Nor did they take evasive maneuvers. They kept pacing the B-17s, seemingly oblivious to the threat.

"Creepy little buggers," Monroe said.

"Can't be a pilot," Blumenkranz said. "You were flying some new secret Nazi aircraft, would you just sit there and let someone photograph you? Do nothing while they lined you up in their sights?"

"I might," Monroe said. "If I was cocky. Or if I couldn't see them. Or if the aircraft I was flying was invincible."

Blumenkranz shook his head. "They're unmanned."

"Nothing is invincible," Smith said.

"You guys gonna start filming or what?" Blumenkranz said. "I don't like sitting here threatening the Kraut Balls but not shooting. Like some target."

"Are the Foo Fighters unmanned?" Monroe said to Major Smith.

Blumenkranz cocked the Browning by pulling the bolt handle on its right side. The handle was wooden and rounded, as if plucked from a giant baker's rolling pin. It was fitted into a long slot that ran half the length of the Browning, rear to middle. The bolt handle's default position was in the center of the gun. Blumenkranz pulled the bolt handle back and it popped forward to its original middle position, creating two ratchety clicks that were the most reassuring sound in the world. Except perhaps the roar of Mustang engines.

Blumenkranz stared at the Kraut Balls, which seemed the size of basketballs because of the distance. Basketballs made of liquid metal. How in the hell could Kraut Balls hover the way they did?

Monroe flipped open his mask, removed his mitten, raised his middle finger, and gave the Kraut Balls the bird. He laughed.

"Eat shit Huns!" he screamed.

Monroe stood for several seconds near the center of the waist gun window, exaggerated smile on his face, middle finger brandished.

No reaction from the Kraut Balls.

"Definitely unmanned," Monroe said.

"Or unarmed," Gassoway said.

"Was a Kraut in there," Blumenkranz said, "he would have shot us for sure."

"Maybe," Kennemer said, "they think flipping the bird means hello."

Monroe closed his mask and put his mitten back on. "Would flick them off longer," he said, "but my finger's getting cold."

"Use your other hand," Blumenkranz said. "Switch hands often enough, they'll stay warm."

Monroe shook his head.

"You're scared," Blumenkranz said. "And I don't blame you."

"Ready to film," McGinnon said.

"Once we start the camera," Smith said, "wait a few seconds until McGinnon gives you the thumbs up. When he does, no joking around, open fire immediately. We can only film for a minute."

"Yes, sir," Blumenkranz said.

McGinnon pressed his face into the Fastax eyepiece and then reached forward and flicked a small switch on the camera housing. It took several seconds to run up to speed, and the whining hum it produced grew steadily higher in pitch as it did, until leveling off. McGinnon engaged the film feed and the shuffling deck sound commenced. He once again worked the lever which swung and pivoted the camera with his right hand and worked the focus with his left. Gears on the camera lens allowed him to adjust it even with mittens on. McGinnon twisted the focus back and forth fractionally.

"Thumbs up," he shouted.

Blumenkranz lined up the leftmost Foo Fighter in his sight and opened fire. He had been trained to fire in short bursts to conserve ammo and prevent overheating of his Browning.

The Browning gyrated back and forth rapidly and roared. About a half dozen rounds raced outward. Blumenkranz stopped firing. He was used to aiming at fighters accelerating towards him at stupendous speeds and compensating for angles and distances that were constantly changing. Picking off a stationary object less than fifty yards off the wing was child's play. Like a field goal kicker making a chip shot, Blumenkranz didn't even need to look to know he'd nailed it. He didn't look away though. This was combat. And it wasn't everyday you got to down a Foo Fighter.

Blumenkranz's aim was true. The fifty-cal rounds approached the center of the leftmost Foo Fighter. They seemed to penetrate the haze surrounding it and slow instantly, as if entering water. Small phosphorescent reddish flares of light then appeared one after another as each bullet entered the haze. The flashes grew larger, seemed to combine into a single larger flash, and then subsided.

All the bullets had hit the Foo Fighter in the exact center.
It was still a hovering silverish orb enclosed in a haze.
And it appeared completely undamaged.

"Holy shit," Blumenkranz said.

"What the hell?" Monroe said.

"Are you fucking kidding me?" Gassoway said.

"Fire again," Smith said. "Longer duration this time. Hurry up!"

"Yes, sir," Blumenkranz said as he opened fire.

The Browning could fire 7-10 rounds per second. Blumenkranz fired for about six seconds, which would be approximately fifty rounds. The firing became a continuous roar overladen with the discrete chuttering of individual rounds. Blumenkranz's body shook as the Browning slammed forward and backward repeatedly. He flexed to resist the movement, keeping the Browning steadied and its aim true.

A stream of bullets once again raced out towards the exact center of the leftmost Foo Fighter. The first few did the exact same thing the previous volley had, becoming phosphorescent reddish flashes as soon as they contacted the haze at the Kraut Ball's exterior.

As additional bullets made contact, the flashes seemed to occur farther inside the haze, closer to the center of the Kraut Ball. They also grew brighter and larger.

Blumenkranz had the sense that the Kraut Ball was encased in transparent flowing gelatin that could regenerate rapidly when pierced. Each bullet pierced its way into the Jell-O a bit, and if you pierced it with enough rounds rapidly, the Jell-O couldn't regenerate fast enough and bullets might penetrate the object inside.

Blumenkranz wasn't sure this impression was correct. Everything was happening quickly, in at most a few seconds, far too quickly to truly assimilate with any degree of confidence or certainty.

The Kraut Ball erupted into a blinding reddish flash. Blumenkranz squinted and closed his eyes reflexively. He heard sizzling static in his interphone, opened his eyes, and the Kraut Ball was plummeting downward. It seemed silverish, but also phosphorescent red.

Blumenkranz couldn't maintain focus on the Kraut Balls because the roar of the two engines on the left wing decreased in volume and pitch and the left-wing tip of *Bachelor's Den* lurched downward about four feet. The aircraft veered left, drifting out of formation.

Blumenkranz flexed his legs and leaned back, adjusting his center of gravity. He had the Browning to support him and stayed standing with relative ease. To his right, Blumenkranz saw Doctor Devlin fall forward, on a trajectory that could send him tumbling out the window. Smith had stabilized himself the way Blumenkranz had and gripped the window ledge with his left arm for support. Without looking away from the Foo Fighters, Smith reached out with his right arm, grabbed the back of Devlin's jacket, yanked him, and held him upright.

Out his peripheral vision, Blumenkranz saw Jablonski lose his balance. He was smart enough to tuck into a semi-fetal position as he fell, and his thick sheepskin shell cushioned his landing. Jablonski cursed repeatedly, but appeared fine, and had the sense to stay down. McGinnon used the camera to stabilize himself and kept his face pressed into the camera eyepiece, focusing on the shot.

Blumenkranz didn't know about the two right props, but the two left props were spinning slowly and seemed destined to stall. The two left engines were making a desperate sputtering sound. Though Blumenkranz's vantage was from the rear of the wing and the props were on the front of it, the portion of the props he could see was becoming less blurry, more visible.

Blumenkranz felt fear but not panic. He had faced death many times in combat and knew that the surest way to succumb was to relinquish calm. If both left engines stalled, *Bachelor's Den* would go down and they would all be joining the Caterpillar Club. Blumenkranz had the sudden realization that if the Nazis learned about Smith's mission they might torture everyone mercilessly. Nazis bitter about the Allies imminent victory might torture everyone even if they didn't learn about the mission.

The engines continued to sputter. Crashing seemed more probable every instant, but there was nothing Blumenkranz could do about it. He found himself peering at the Kraut Balls.

The Kraut Balls followed the wing tip when it lurched downward. But not uniformly. The lead Kraut Ball closest to the wing tip moved with it, descending to maintain the same altitude as the tip and constant separation. The Kraut Balls behind the lead also descended, but not as much as the lead. Overall, the motion of the Kraut Balls seemed like an optical illusion, as if they were navigation lights on some triangular aircraft that had banked while also shrinking.

Blumenkranz usually tried not to envision his death during a bombing run, but Kraut Balls seemed to shatter all the rules. Blumenkranz saw his mother at his funeral, standing amid a sky of corn stalks, bawling uncontrollably.

Fifty-cal rounds were still rushing in above the Kraut Balls, at the space where the leftmost Kraut Ball had been, but they were no longer a continuous stream. The bullets that had been frontmost were gone. Destroyed by the flash or explosion?

Except it didn't seem like a typical explosion. No turbulence had been created, and no shrapnel had flown towards the waist gun window or pelted the fuselage. Such sounds were unmistakable. And no one was hurt. The left wing and engines were also not maimed. No engine was smoking. And the wing had no abrasions or holes, not even dents.

The two right engines roared more loudly as Ostrye maximized their power to compensate. He simultaneously lowered the left aileron. On the rear of the wing, a hinged flap rotated and pointed downward slightly.

But only a little bit.

Presumably, the aileron on the right wing that Blumenkranz couldn't see was also being raised.

But only a little bit.

This correction had its intended effect of creating more lift under the left wing and presumably less lift under the right. *Bachelor's Den* rolled rightward on its central front-to-back axis, like a doorknob being turned, until level.

Unfortunately, but unavoidably, *Bachelor's Den* also rotated counterclockwise on its top-to-bottom or sky-to-ground axis, like a top being spun. It was similar to a car that twisted while hydroplaning, continuing movement in a forward direction despite being angled sideways. This sensation of yaw was one of the most petrifying experiences in a plane. It was as if the plane were on ice skates attempting a jump stop.

Blumenkranz's body became a banjo string. He felt his stomach lurch and his guts seemed to hiccup inside him. Breath billowed through the spaces between his teeth and out his compressed lips.

Blumenkranz knew that when a plane rolled without banking, yaw resulted in the direction opposite the roll. If a plane rolled too aggressively, yaw could spin the aircraft so fast that it was torn apart or dropped out of the sky. This is why Ostrye had been sparing with his aileron corrections.

Blumenkranz imagined *Bachelor's Den* spinning faster and plummeting downwards. Spinning too fast for a bail out. No Caterpillar Club. Blumenkranz would feel his guts slamming upwards towards his Adam's apple as he prepared to meet his maker. The rapidly accelerating spin would make him nauseous and blur his vision. *Bachelor's Den* would fall faster and faster, spin quicker and quicker, like some masochistic carnival ride—until it stopped instantaneously and Blumenkranz ended.

Ostrye quickly corrected the yaw, presumably by adjusting the rudder that protruded vertically at the rear of the plane. This effect was little different than hanging an oar out the back of a canoe to steer it.

Blumenkranz once again endured the discomforting sensation of the plane skidding, this time in the opposite direction, clockwise. His innards lurched less severely, a sock to the gut by an amateur rather than Sugar Ray Robinson.

The skid stabilized and *Bachelor's Den* once again faced straight ahead. Though less nervous, Blumenkranz was hardly comforted, for he knew that *Bachelor's Den* was now a precarious configuration of counterbalanced forces. It was almost dragging itself through the air rather than flying through it. This murdered fuel efficiency, strained the aircraft, and stressed the pilot, who would have to make split-second adjustments to the engines, ailerons, and rudder if changing conditions such as wind or weather unbalanced the counterbalanced forces. If Ostrye was just a split second slow or miscalculated in making adjustments to a complex set of difficult-to-assess force interactions, then *Bachelor's Den* would crash and they would all die or end up tortured by Nazis.

It was far safer to have the plane flying normally, but Ostrye had also done some impressive piloting.

Damn impressive.

Not many pilots could make such corrections so quickly without sacrificing altitude and speed or banking, and being forced to drop completely out of formation. Once you were out of formation, you were a gazelle separated from the herd. The lions of the plain, the Fucking Wolves, would move in and devour you. *Bachelor's Den* was no longer tightly in formation off *Dog Breath's* wing, but it hadn't dropped completely out of formation either.

Thank God Ostrye was their Captain!

Blumenkranz wondered if Major Smith could have done as well but didn't get very far in this rumination because the Kraut Balls readjusted to the new wing position. The motion was a reverse of before, with the lead Kraut Ball moving upward and outward, maintaining the same altitude as the wing tip and the same separation. The other Kraut Balls once again followed the lead of the first Kraut Ball, though the motion still appeared like the simultaneous synchronized motion of all Kraut Balls at once.

Blumenkranz couldn't help thinking of an accordion. The Kraut Balls seemed like some three-dimensional accordion. When this accordion was contracted or expanded, it decreased or increased the separation between all Kraut Balls simultaneously, in all three dimensions.

Blumenkranz didn't have time to ponder this assessment or its implications deeply. It was momentary and fragmented.

The static in the interphone vanished suddenly.

"Course the ailerons were neutral," Ostrye said. "Doing my best to limit the adverse yaw. We're not anywhere near stall velocity. That can't be it. And I don't think changing the fuel mix is going to do diddly. No. No. Dammit Gassoway. I told you. Only thing I saw was a huge spike in my ammeter up t—"

"The problem is not the fuel mix," Devlin said. "I would expect that if we are just patient the problem will self correct in a moment or tw—"

The left engines began spinning more rapidly. The left-wing tip drifted upward as they did, and the Kraut Balls rose with it. *Bachelor's Den* moved back into formation. Ostrye raised the left aileron gradually to coincide with the ramping up of the engines, and presumably also adjusted the right aileron and the rudder. The roar of the right engines also diminished. Ostrye's adjustments were expert, but the left wing nonetheless vacillated up and down a bit as he made them, and the Kraut Balls moved up and down with it, responding instantaneously each time.

Blumenkranz sighed deeply. Tension ebbed out of him like heat, but also persisted.

Finally the aileron was completely retracted and everything was back to normal. *Bachelor's Den* returned to its left echelon Deputy Lead position tight off *Dog Breath's* wing. The Kraut Balls were close to their original position before Blumenkranz had fired, though still with less separation than originally.

"There we go," Devlin said pleasantly. "Now that wasn't so bad, was it?"

Jablonksi stood and looked at Devlin like he wanted to kill him. Blumenkranz couldn't help chuckling. You just couldn't ever tell about people. Blumenkranz would have figured Devlin was the biggest coward of the bunch, but the nerd seemed remarkably unperturbed.

"The angular electrostatic momentum was indeed profuse," Devlin said in his nasal voice. "I was afraid of that."

Smith glanced over at Devlin with a dry expression, shook his head ever so slightly, and then peered over the window edge at the downed Kraut Ball.

15

The turret allowed Tucker a panoramic, bird's-eye view of the world below the bomber, and he obtained a vantage of the Kraut Balls which the rest of the crew couldn't. He watched the burning Kraut Ball accelerate downward like a plummeting meteor. Except that it seemed slowed down to about one-half normal speed.

A cross between a meteor and a balloon?

How the hell was that even possible?

How the hell was any of this even possible?

"Seeing anything different from underneath?" Smith said.

Tucker summarized the slow fall.

Smith didn't seem surprised in the least.

"Crashing Kraut Ball's got a fire trail," Tucker said. "Know that's expected for downed planes, but since Kraut Balls don't seem to be planes and don't have any exhaust or engines, just thought I'd mention it."

"Excellent," Smith said. "Precisely the kind of observations we need. What else?"

"Fire trail doesn't look like fire exactly," Tucker said. "Not like a fire from wood or oil or what not. I've had a front row seat for the burning of a slew of fighters and bombers. This looks different. Like a flare."

The onrushing wind blew the Kraut Ball backward, and it fell away behind Tucker. Tucker used his two hand controls to rotate the turret and get a better view. The azimuth control in his left hand rotated the turret 360 degrees, and the elevation control in his right hand swiveled it up or down 90 degrees. Combinations of these two movements allowed a complete range of motion, and Tucker was adept enough that he used both hand controls at once. The hydraulics pumped and the motors whirred as he swiveled.

Tucker peered out the porthole between his legs at the downed Kraut Ball. It was becoming too small to see. There was nothing more to report about it. Tucker repositioned his turret facing upward and leftward. He saw a portion of the underside of the B-17, including the wing. And the six silverish Kraut Balls just off it. Translucent sheaths encased them. The sheaths seemed to wobble or undulate.

"The shimmering surrounding the Kraut Balls reminds me of the desert," Tucker said. "The way heat haze makes things fuzzy. Objects behind the shimmery heat blur sometimes seem like they're moving. But they aren't. It's the shimmer that's undulating. Maybe the Kraut Balls aren't moving either. Maybe what's encasing them is moving, but they aren't."

"The Kraut Balls are moving 182 miles an hour," Ostrye said. "Keeping up with us."

"I mean spinning," Tucker said. "Wobbling. Undulating. Whatever you call it."

"Resonating," Devlin said. "Are the resonations thicker or denser in any one direction?"

Tucker swiveled his turret to get a better view.

"Denser near the front," he said. "In the direction of movement. Maybe. Can't be sure on that. Also, it almost seems like the undulations are . . . they're . . . synchronized. Like dancers or something.

Like the wobbling of all the Kraut Balls is marching to the same beat."

"Damn I wish we had a Fastax down there," Smith said.

"Dream on," Tucker said. "I don't even have room for a Brownie."

16

Once he could no longer see the descending Kraut Ball and he con-
cluded his conversation with Tucker, Smith approached McGinnon. McGinnon was still filming, face pressed into the eye piece.
"Tell me you got all that," Smith said.

"I did," McGinnon said. "Even got some footage of the downed
Kraut Ball. When the plane rolled. We got lucky there again."

"The plane rolled because we lost engines one and two," Ostrye
said. "That's not my idea of luck."

"Probably better if we'd crashed," Gassoway said. "You could
have filmed the fucking Foo Fighter the whole way down."

Smith had the photographers move a Fastax from the nose to
the waist gun compartment and did his best to tune out Gassoway's
pissing and moaning. Even a crash probably wouldn't shut the bastard up. If they died, Smith felt sure he'd get to hell and find Gassoway there complaining. Gassoway and Kennemer together. Gassoway complaining, and Kennemer preaching his pussified pacifism.
Having to listen to those two for eternity would be the very defi-
nition of hell.

Your duty was your duty and you had to do it. They might very well die in the next hour. Smith wasn't any more excited about this prospect than Gassoway or Kennemer. He just didn't see the point of whining about it.

17

Monroe was peering intently out the left waist gun window. His eyes were frantic. Overwhelmed.

"I don't get it," he said. "We killed one of the Kraut Balls. But they didn't take evasive maneuvers or attack. If they know we can kill them, why would they just sit there?"

"They always do that," Blumenkranz said. "Most every crew that ever saw one says the same thing."

"Kraut Balls have to think they can kill us," Monroe said. "How many crews didn't live to report what we're experiencing? Or about to experience."

"Maybe Kraut Balls are kind of like Trojan horses," Kennemer said.

"Like land mines," Gassoway said. "But in the sky."

"A sky mine," Forrest said. "Or air mine."

"That's probably why we're always told never to engage Foo Fighters," Gassoway said. "Maybe they can only attack when attacked."

"If that were true," Monroe said, "attacking them would be the worst thing we could do."

"We're going to shoot another Kraut Ball," Major Smith said.

The interphone silence said more than any belly aching could have.

"Wait just a minute," Ostrye said.

"We don't have a minute," Smith said. "We have no idea how long the Kraut Balls will continue ghosting us."

Monroe's eyes became hollow and vacant. He gulped hard.

"I don't mind taking my chances against fighters and flak," he said. "But this is like suicide."

Smith stared right into Monroe's eyes.

"Mines explode," he said. "The Kraut Ball didn't."

"It didn't explode like a normal bomb," Monroe said, "but it created some other kind of explosion that stalled our engines."

"We recovered from that stall," Smith said.

"That doesn't mean we'll recover from the next one."

"Maybe not," Smith said.

"So I'm supposed to maybe die," Monroe said. "So that you can photograph another Kraut Ball being downed."

"Precisely," Smith said.

Monroe stood motionless for a long moment. His eyes seemed to relax yet harden. Then he shrugged. Monroe approached Blumenkranz and raised his mittens. They high fived, their mittens thumped, and the sound was swallowed by the engine.

Monroe said, "Let's kill these Kraut motherfuckers."

"I want everyone to make sure they're wearing their safety harnesses," Ostrye said. "And they have their chutes."

"Agreed," Smith said.

Ostrye had everyone sound off one by one, confirming they had their parachutes and safety harnesses and were ready to bail if need be. Jablonski and the chubby photographer had questions about bailout procedures. Ostrye answered them quickly but patiently.

Blumenkranz pitied the fear in the photographer's voices. He didn't ever want to sound like that. Like a coward.

"Everyone ready?" Smith said.

Everyone was.

Kennemer spoke in an abnormally nasal voice.

"Let's just hope," he said, "that the angular electrostatic momentum isn't too profuse."

18

Blumenkranz peered out his window at the silverish Kraut Balls. Six of them in vee formation, still right off the wing.

Hovering.

Shimmering.

Stalking.

Blumenkranz grabbed the handles of his old friend Browning and steeled himself.

Fucking Kraut bastards.

He was going to take the fight to them this time for sure.

And if he had to join the Caterpillar Club doing so, so be it. Blumenkranz slapped his shoulder holster, felt the pistol there. He'd kill a few Krauts on the ground, too. Go out fighting.

McGinnon started the third Fastax.

"Thumbs up," he screamed.

Blumenkranz fired fifty rounds at the leftmost Kraut Ball, just like the first time. It was still the easiest shot a waist gunner could ever imagine. A stream of bullets raced straight towards the exact center of the leftmost Kraut Ball.

The process of the rounds gradually penetrating the transparent gelatin sheath of the Kraut Balls was repeated. Reddish phosphorescent splashes of increasing size and intensity began to appear.

And then the sheath vanished suddenly, revealing a momentary, teasing glimpse of solid metal underneath. Shiny metal. Silverish still, but also with a grayish quality. Was it naturally shiny, or was that sunlight reflecting? There wasn't time to tell because the Kraut Ball accelerated downward.

It was that lightning fast acceleration the Kraut Ball had utilized when first approaching *Bachelor's Den*. The Kraut Ball seemed to disappear and then reappear about ten yards below where it had been. The bullets that should have been hitting it were encountering empty sky and racing past the Foo Fighter formation.

Blumenkranz was learning to expect the unexpected with Kraut Balls. Except this movement wasn't even unexpected, as he'd seen it before. Blumenkranz nonetheless did a doubletake and still had to fight the subconscious reaction that his eyes were playing tricks on him.

They were not.

Peering at the descending Kraut Ball, Blumenkranz thought he saw a solid metallic object. It looked spherical. Or at least damn near spherical. But he also thought he saw flatness for an instant.

So it seemed.

Was anything about Kraut Balls what it seemed?

Blumenkranz only viewed the solid Kraut Ball for a moment. A tantalizing moment.

Then the encasing haze returned and the Kraut Ball vanished under the belly of the bomber.

19

Tucker swiveled the turret so he could observe the westward trajectory of the falling Kraut Ball. No fire trail this time. And the Kraut Ball fell much more slowly, as if sinking through water. It also wasn't blown backward by onrushing wind as much as the previous Kraut Ball. Was it still generating partial upward and forward thrust somehow? The fuzzy sheath which encased the Kraut Ball undulated more intensely, growing thicker and thinner than it had previously, which caused it to become extremely blurry and then almost visible repeatedly.

The Kraut Ball shot upward diagonally towards *Bachelor's Den* and the other Kraut Balls, followed them from behind for a few seconds, and then flashed and became whitish. It seemed like lightning was trapped inside the fuzzy sheath. Numerous small bolts spread throughout the entire surface area like fissures appearing in a cracking rock. Was the lightning trapped between the outer hull of the silver sphere and the containment haze, racing around?

Tucker's eyes bulged and he froze. It couldn't be that simple. Could it? If it was that simple, then

Then what?

Tucker didn't know. But he was suddenly seized by a strong desire for ignorance. He didn't want to be one of the people who possessed such a simple secret. Somehow, the sheer simplicity made it seem more dangerous to know.

The lightning persisted a mere instant and vanished, leaving the pulsating, translucent sheath. The silver orb began darting around impossibly fast, performing hard 90 degree turns, tracing out curves, zig zags, figure eights, other more whimsical contours, as if it were the brush of some manic and perhaps schizophrenic painter. The darting orb was no longer keeping up with the squadron and was shrinking as *Bachelor's Den* raced away from it.

"It almost looked like ele—"

Tucker paused.

"Like what?" Smith said.

Like electricity. Like it was electrical. Like it got shorted out or hit by lightning.

Doctor Devlin had mentioned angles of electrosomething spinnamajig, or whatever it was. But Tucker had clearly heard the word electro.

"Not sure what it looked like, sir," Tucker said. "Was going to say elliptical. Like it wasn't totally spherical. But I think that was a trick of the light or undulations or whatever. I don't know. Thing's a total mystery to me."

The Kraut Ball flashed with lightning again, lightning more intense and of shorter duration than previously. The sheath encasing it vanished. It was unquestionably a sphere now. A simple, silverish-gray, metallic sphere. Except for a brief instant Tucker thought he saw flatness, as if the Kraut Ball was the shape of a pistol bullet with most of the rear lopped off. The sphere—if it was a sphere—plummeted straight down like a bomb dropped out of a plane. Tucker squinted, tried to see details of the metallic hull, but it was too distant. He watched the Kraut Ball vanish from sight and then kept quiet.

20

In the waist gunner compartment, the Fastax was making its characteristic shuffling card sound.

"About twenty five seconds of film left," McGinnon said.

"See if you can shoot just behind the haze encasing a Kraut Ball," Smith said to Blumenkranz.

Blumenkranz hesitated. Only five Kraut Balls remained, the lead directly off the wing, one just left of the lead, and three right of the lead. They were still in vee formation, like an arrow tip pointed at the side of the bomber.

Blumenkranz couldn't shoot at the three Kraut Balls right of the lead. They were in front of the engines, and if they exploded, shrapnel might enter the engine. Also, such a shot would require bullets to cross directly over the wing and dangerously close to the prop. No way was Blumenkranz chancing such a shot, no matter what Smith said. Smith seemed too smart to make such a request regardless.

The lead Kraut Ball directly off the wing was also a dangerous shot. If Blumenkranz's aim drifted even a little right or downward, he'd shoot the engine or the wing. That probably wasn't going to happen, but it was also a risk better avoided.

That left one Kraut Ball. But even it was closer to the wing than Blumenkranz would have preferred. The other Kraut Balls he'd shot had been farther out in formation, farther away from the wing. If this Kraut Ball exploded, it would almost certainly destroy part of the wing and cripple or down *Bachelor's Den*.

"That Kraut Ball," Blumenkranz said, "is awfully close to the wing."

"You don't say," Smith said.

"You sure you want me to shoot?"

"That's why I gave the order."

"Yes, sir."

Smith pointed to the sky behind the leftmost Kraut Ball.

"Left of it," he said. "Don't hit the Kraut Ball itself. Or the haze that encases it. Aim right behind the haze."

"Left behind you mean."

"Right," Smith said. "We clear?"

"Crystal, sir."

Blumenkranz flexed the gun tightly to limit recoil and drift. He squatted so his face was just above the barrel and about a foot behind it. Blumenkranz peered into the sight on the front of the weapon, which resembled a monocle with crosshairs, and finalized his aim.

He opened fire. The Browning roared and rocked back and forth. Bullets raced outward. Their trajectory was several yards behind the Kraut Ball.

Blumenkranz had missed wide purposely, to calibrate his aim. He adjusted his aim rightward fractionally and fired another quick burst. The trajectory was closer, only a couple yards behind the Kraut Ball.

"About fifteen seconds of film left," McGinnon said.

Blumenkranz adjusted his aim rightward fractionally one final time and fired. The Browning roared. Bullets flew exactly where Smith wanted them, just behind the translucent sheath. Except when they drew near it, they glowed phosphorescent red, accelerated as if being sucked into a drain, circled around the outside edge of the Kraut Ball, disappeared behind it, and then raced off away from it.

It was as if they'd been fired from a different initial trajectory and had gone through the Kraut Ball. This hadn't happened. But looking at the bullets moving away behind the Kraut Ball, that was what it seemed like.

Blumenkranz gaped at Smith, who was nonchalant.

"What the fuck?" Monroe said. "Over?"

"Fire again!" Smith said. "Until we're out of film."

Blumenkranz obeyed. This time he didn't let go of the trigger. The Browning burped out a steady stream of bullets at its maximum rate of about ten per second. They all followed the same trajectory as the first, were whisked around the Kraut Ball, vanished behind it, and then raced away from it.

Blumenkranz couldn't fire indefinitely or his Browning would overheat and seize up. He also needed some ammo for the run. He stopped firing.

"Less than ten seconds of film," McGinnon said.

"How is that possible?" Monroe said.

"Like light beams deflected around a star," Devlin said.

"Fire again!" Smith said.

Blumenkranz continued firing. *Bachelor's Den* hit a pocket of turbulence as he did, lurching forward. This redirected the trajectory of Blumenkranz's shots rightward. He adjusted leftward almost instantly, but this still took almost a second, and several rounds were thus fired towards the rear section of the Kraut Ball's hull rather than behind it. These bullets were no longer whisked around the Kraut Ball, but hit it, penetrating the haze incrementally as before.

Blumenkranz glanced at his shoulder, at the pull ring for his chute, and then steeled himself for the stalling engines.

The Kraut Ball's translucent sheath seemed to fill with lightning for a brief instant. The lightning vanished suddenly and the Kraut Ball became a slightly blurry silver sphere for an instant. The translucent sheath then returned, but it seemed to expand and contract rhythmically, as if two translucent spheres of different size were being rapidly and repeatedly swapped. The Kraut Ball fell from formation and begin to slowly descend, much slower than its two downed predecessors.

The bullets that should have hit the Kraut Ball were deflected upward and over it, like a car riding over a bump, and sped away from it. The Kraut Ball was descending, and seemed to drag bullets with it as it redirected their trajectory, though they flew straight once past it. The rounds thus approached the Kraut Ball at one height, exited behind it at a lower height, but seemed to be curving upward over the Kraut Ball in the interim.

Blumenkranz once again fought the sense that he was observing an impossibility. Foo Fighter exploits might seem like an optical illusion, but they weren't aeronautical sleight-of-hand. Everything was simply happening so fast it exceeded human sensory capabilities. If Blumenkranz could barely see what was happening, how could Foo Fighter pilots, if there were any, possibly react fast enough to be of any use? Was that why they just sat there?

Blumenkranz wasn't sure exactly what he'd seen or was seeing. And there wasn't time to figure it out. The Kraut Ball was drifting downward and the rounds Blumenkranz had fired were racing into the air where it had been, at a succession of different heights that his eyes told him were impossible.

Blumenkranz had a desperate desire to slow things down and get a better look.

What had Devlin said?

Many seemingly mysterious phenomena become understandable when viewed in slow motion.

Blumenkranz glanced at the Fastax.

Five thousand frames per second.

The reason high-speed cameras were needed was now abundantly obvious. Blumenkranz desperately wanted to see the Fastax film, but knew with depressing certainty he never would.

21

Bachelor's Den was part of a box formation containing 54 bombers and many were behind and below it. The Kraut Ball was falling slowly towards the nose of one of these onrushing bombers. Tucker had a curdling view of the procession.

"Possible impact of the Kraut Ball with a friendly!" he said.

"Where?" Blumenkranz said. "We can't see shit."

"We can't see it either," Ostrye said.

"Neither can we," Artipo said.

"Wish we could film it," Smith said.

"I can see it," Kennemer said. "Gonna be close."

Tucker swiveled his turret and angled it downward to keep the Kraut Ball in view. Its movement reminded him of a slowly deflating balloon which might take a quarter hour to reach the ground. The Kraut Ball sauntered downward and rearward, straight towards the nose of an onrushing B-17. It looked like *Deuces Wild*, but Tucker couldn't be sure.

Deuces Wild veered left to avoid the Kraut Ball. As it did, the Kraut Ball came in just behind its right wing. *Deuces Wild* would have hit the B-17 next to it, but that B-17 veered left. The engines of both aircraft made high-pitched whines as they strained.

While there was room between bomber elements, space for evasive maneuvers within each element was limited, especially in the horizontal plane of each vee formation. The vee formation the Kraut Ball displaced was tight and by the book, with only fifty feet of separation between wingtips of adjacent bombers. It was a miracle the Flying Fortresses avoided a collision.

"Tell us what the hell is happening!" McIntire said.

"Those are some lucky SOBs," Kennemer said.

"Not just luck," Tucker said. "Ballsy piloting."

"Kraut Ballsy," Kennemer said.

No one laughed.

The Kraut Ball drifted downward, towards the lead bomber of another flight of bombers. The lead bomber took evasive action and veered left, like the previous lead had. The pilot in the B-17 left of the lead bomber didn't react quickly enough. He didn't veer left immediately.

The bombers smashed into each other wings first. The outermost props of the two aircraft contacted, sparked, and the clattering of metal on metal rang out. Nothing penetrated the roar of *Bachelor's Den's* engines easily, and though the grinding props sounded more distant than they were, they were nonetheless a sickening sound that no airmen ever wanted to hear.

The interlocked props seemed to fuse together momentarily and the Siamese planes banked towards each other, both becoming vertical as their contacted wings dipped downward. Their cockpits smashed together and erupted in flames. The Siamese aircraft fell backward, spun out of control, began slow, gentle flips, and smashed into a B-17 at the rear of a different element.

All three Flying Fortresses exploded. Each had about 1300 gallons of fuel remaining, meaning 3,900 gallons of fuel ignited instantly. A monstrous fireball roared upward, and as the charred bombers dropped out of the sky, a conspicuous cloud of thick, black smoke billowed from them.

"Could see that plume in Tokyo," Gassoway said. "Be real hard for Kraut fighters to locate us now."

"Krauts already know we're here," Ostrye said.

"Why leave it to chance though," Gassoway said. "Right, Major Smith? Nazis won't launch the aircraft you need to observe and film if they don't know we're here."

The silence on the interphone was gaping.

"Not worried about a few thousand dead airmen," Gassoway said, "long as you get your pictures. That the lay of it?"

"Your whining won't make us any safer, Sergeant Gassoway."

"I wasn't whining."

"Course you weren't," Smith said.

The Kraut Ball fell away from the formation and continued its gentle descent, unharmed. The plummeting of the three bombers seemed disturbingly rapid by comparison.

The left wing of *Deuces Wild* was leaning downward slightly. Engine one, its leftmost, was spinning more slowly, and the prop was more visible, less blurry. The right props spun more quickly as the aircraft adjusted for the reduced power from engine one.

"Kraut Ball caused engine problems in the friendly it almost hit," Tucker said. "Pretty sure it's *Deuces Wild*."

"Probably disturbed the airflow in front of the prop," Ostrye said. "She'll right herself."

"Came in behind the wing, sir."

Silence. A lack of conversation anyway. The B-17 engines still roared with fury.

Deuces Wild's engine one began spinning at full speed again.

"You were right, sir," Tucker said. "She recovered and is righting herself."

"Kraut Ball probably just disturbed the airflow in front of the aircraft a bit during its approach," Ostrye said. "Could do that even if it dropped behind the wing."

"Yeah," Tucker said. "That must be it."

22

Blumenkranz flipped his mask open, revealing an expression of dawning horror. There was an emptiness in his eyes.

"God forgive me," he said. "I just murdered thirty Americans."

"This isn't an Agatha Christie novel," Smith said. "You didn't murder anyone."

"I shot the Kraut Ball."

"Yes you did," Smith said.

"And it caused the planes to blow up."

"Yes it did," Smith said.

"So I killed thirty airmen."

"You'd make a good journalist," Smith said. "Got a knack for summarizing the obvious."

"Those airmen's deaths are my fault."

Smith shook his head back and forth slowly.

"Stop being ridiculous," he said. "You can't ascribe simplistic causality or blame for deaths in the chaos of war."

"You gave the order to shoot the Kraut Ball," Monroe said to Smith. "It's your fault, too."

"Sure," Smith said in a monotone. "Entirely my fault." He glanced at Blumenkranz. "Feel better?"

"No. Those airmen didn't deserve to die."

Smith shrugged. "Who does?"

"The fucking Krauts," Monroe said.

"You don't even give a shit about the airmen we just killed," Blumenkranz said. "Would you give a shit if we all died?"

"I didn't want those bomber crews to die," Smith said. "Nor am I insensitive to the loss. But I'm also not going to sit around crying about outcomes I can't control or couldn't control. If we don't focus on our mission, we'll all die."

"Doesn't killing friendlies upset you?" Blumenkranz said.

"I've killed friendlies," Smith said. "And even one friend. But soldiers shouldn't snivel like housewives. Blame is mental masturbation."

The emptiness vacated Blumenkranz's eyes. Some of his usual exuberance seemed to have returned. Smith put his arm around Blumenkranz's shoulder, shook him affectionately, looked him in the eyes, and conveyed candid respect. They watched the Kraut Balls together.

"Ever hear of Giulio Douhet?" Smith said.

"My air tactics instructor mentioned him during training," Ostrye said. "But I forgot what he did."

"Speaking to Sergeant Blumenkranz," Smith said.

"Sorry," Ostrye said.

"Douhet was an Italian General and air power theorist," Smith said. "He's one of the inventors of the doctrine of strategic bombing."

"Remind me to shit on his grave," Gassoway said.

"I'll tell my secretary," Smith said. He looked at Blumenkranz. "The war isn't won."

"It'll be over soon though," Blumenkranz said.

"Maybe it will, maybe it won't. Till you've won a war, you can always lose it. History is replete with overconfident armies that snatched defeat from the jaws of victory. America will not make that mistake."

"What are the Kraut Balls for?" Blumenkranz said.

"Exactly," Smith said. "Douhet said that victory smiles upon those who anticipate the changes in the character of war, not upon those who wait to adapt themselves after the changes occur."

"So Kraut Balls are a change in the character of war?" Blumenkranz said.

"Are you stupid?" Smith said.

"No."

"Then think before you speak and don't say stupid things. Look at the Kraut Balls and think about what you've seen them do. Your question answers itself."

"But Kraut Balls are German," Blumenkranz said. "Ain't they?"

"Hate to have to rename them."

"That would mean we're the ones adapting ourselves after the changes occur."

"The change is still occurring," Smith said. "Just beginning actually. But yes, we did begin adapting later than our foes."

"So does that mean Germany has anticipated the change in the character in war? That victory will smile upon them?"

"Good question."

23

The translucent sheath encasing the frontmost Kraut Ball had begun to undulate more intensely and erratically, and it was drifting up and down sporadically rather than maintaining a steady heading like the other Kraut Balls. McGinnon was filming the behavior from the left waist-gun window, and the other three photographers were moving a camera from the nose to the waist-gun compartment. Space was limited, the camera was heavy, and the cold remained an adversary. The photographers struggled mightily, especially in the crawlway, but finally placed the camera down next to McGinnon.

Jablonski wiped sweat from his brow. "Fifty below zero in here and I'm sweating," he said. "This is asinine."

"I'm parched," the pudgy photographer next to him said.

"This altitude'll do it," Blumenkranz said. "Mountain climbers drink lots of water, and they aren't usually much higher than us."

"Got any Cokes?" the pudgy photographer asked.

Laughter filled the interphone.

"Coke machine's right in the bomb bay," Gassoway said. "Have trouble finding it, just open the doors."

The crew laughed harder.

Until the translucent sheath encasing the Kraut Ball vanished suddenly. The Kraut Ball became a plain silver sphere which was visible for a tantalizing instant before falling and being blown backward by onrushing wind. It appeared smooth, and seemed to spin as it fell, like a rolling ball. It fell rapidly, at a normal rate, as fast as the three bombers.

"Weird the way it falls," Blumenkranz said. "Doesn't career up and down like a bomb when you first release it. Or twist or roll or flip like a fighter or B-17 when hit."

"It is a sphere," Kennemer said. "Symmetrical."

"Duh," Blumenkranz said. "Nothing for the wind to blow like wings."

"The same aerodynamic profile in the X, Y, and Z planes," Kennemer said. "In every direction no matter which way it is facing or spinning. A sphere is the only three-dimensional shape with this property."

"Is that why Krauts made Kraut Balls spherical?" Blumenkranz said.

"As opposed to cubical Kraut Balls?" Devlin said.

"Has anyone ever kicked your ass, Doctor Devlin?" Gassoway said.

"You're not the first to request the privilege," Smith said. "And you won't be the last. But it's not gonna happen on my watch. Tell me you filmed that glimpse of the metallic hull."

"Yep," McGinnon said.

"How long it last?" Smith said.

"Quarter second max."

"And when we play the film back normal speed?"

"Shit," McGinnon said. "I can't do the math."

"Doctor Devlin," Smith said. "Do the math."

"Be happy to. If you'll give me the math."

"Fastax records at five thousand frames per second," McGinnon said. "Commercial thirty-five millimeter projectors like those in movie theatres play at about twenty-five frames per second."

"Elementary," Devlin said. "At 5,000 frames per second, a quarter second is 1,250 frames filmed. 1,250 frames of film replayed at 25 frames per second would take 50 seconds to play completely."

"Holy shit," Blumenkranz said. "That little flash of the Kraut Ball hull we saw will be played back for almost a minute?"

"Yep," McGinnon said. "Assuming there's no math errors."

"I don't make math errors," Devlin said. "Not even light headed at 23,000 feet."

"If the Norden goes out," Artipo said, "I'm going to have Doctor Devlin compute the bomb trajectories."

"Don't know how well I can operate a slide rule in mittens," Devlin said. "Otherwise it wouldn't be a problem."

Smith rolled his eyes.

"If a quarter second of filming takes fifty seconds to play back," Blumenkranz said, "how long would a full sixty-four second reel take to play back?"

Devlin answered instantly. "12,800 seconds. Which is 213 minutes, or 3.55 hours."

Blumenkranz and Ostrye's eyes dilated.

"Three and a half hours?" Blumenkranz said. "You gotta be shitting me?"

"Three point five five hours," Devlin said. "Not three and a half."

"Any way you anal it," Blumenkranz said, "that's a long ass time. Hope you spooks got a popcorn maker."

Smith laughed.

"And there's six rolls," Monroe said. "So that's like nineteen hours."

"21.3 hours," Devlin said.

"That is so bonkers," Blumenkranz said. "Six minutes of film will take twenty one point three hours to play back."

"6 minutes and 24 seconds of film," Devlin said. "Not 6 minutes."

"Doctor Devlin can't possibly have a girlfriend," Gassoway said.

"She's a linguist and anthropologist," Devlin said. "I correct her imprecise mathematics, she corrects my language."

"Match made in heaven," Gassoway said. "Sex must be real precise."

"McGinnon," Devlin said. "Be sure to film the Kraut Balls simply flying next to the squadron for an extended period of time."

"Got at least twenty seconds of that on each roll," McGinnon said. "An eternity."

"Longer," Devlin said. "Glad we captured crashes, accelerations, and other kinetic footage, but we can't neglect the mundane. We need one full roll of the Kraut Balls simply flying."

"You're the boss, Doctor," McGinnon said. "Whatever you want, you got it. Want me to film it now?"

"Yes. As soon as possible."

McGinnon cooked the roll he was filming, and then filmed another full roll, which also had to be moved in from the nose compartment. The filming was uneventful, and they had now used all their Fastaxes except one.

The photographers began the arduous task of moving the expended cameras to the bomb bay. The pudgy photographer asked Smith if the gunners and other airmen could help. He eyed Monroe, who was quite muscular, as he made the request.

"This isn't a union-scale Hollywood shoot," Smith said. "You fucking lard ass. All the gunners are staying at their stations to engage Jerry when he finally makes a showing. Don't ask other people to pay the price for your pastries and dunkers. Now waddle your fat ass back there and help get those cameras moved. Be quick about it and try not to trip on your chins."

The pudgy cameraman waddled off. As he did, Blumenkranz & Monroe laughed hysterically. Laughter soon filled the interphone. It would have been better if the source of levity had been something nobler, but God it felt good to laugh.

24

Smith informed Captain Ostrye that he and Devlin would be unreachable on interphone for a stretch and were not to be disturbed for trivialities. Smith and Devlin unplugged from the ship interphone system and plugged into a rectangular junction box with four interphone ports. It was not standard issue on B-17 bombers and had been created specially by Boeing. The junction box allowed private conversations using interphone microphones and headphones. Though Blumenkranz & Monroe were but feet away, they would be unable to hear Smith and Devlin so long as they kept their oxygen masks on and did not speak loudly.

Smith plugged a heated tape recorder into the junction box. Like the Fastax cameras, it was self-enclosed and single use. Rewind and fast forward were impossible. There were but two buttons, a green one to start recording and a red one to stop it. Also an indicator light.

Smith and Devlin stood next to Blumenkranz and watched the Foo Fighters. They were still silver orbs, still encased in an undulating haze, and still maintained their position off the bomber wing with ease. There were four Foo Fighters remaining, two right of the lead and one left of it.

Smith said, "Blumenkranz has a tiny gigglestick that all the dollies laugh at."

Blumenkranz continued scanning the sky vigilantly.

Smith said, "Monroe couldn't get lucky if you rolled him in gold dust and locked him in a poor house."

Monroe continued watching the Foo Fighters.

"B&M definitely can't hear us," Smith said, "or they'd be giving me an earful for sure."

Devlin nodded. "Should we have kept additional cameras in reserve?"

"A Foo in the hand is worth two in the clouds," Smith said. "Don't like the idea of coming home with unused cameras. And we don't want cameras clusterfucking the gunners once we reach IP or we might not make it home."

"Feels like absolute zero," Devlin said. "My blood is turning into glycerin."

"The cold's the cold. Deal with it."

"And this altitude! I'm lightheaded even with oxygen."

"The altitude's the altitude. Deal with it. I'm as tolerant of weakness as you are stupidity."

"Touché," Devlin said.

Smith imagined himself throwing Devlin out the waist-gunner window. Devlin was such a scrawny wimp he probably wouldn't even fall, but rather would blow around like a piece of paper.

Why couldn't the Office of Scientific Research and Development have found a less annoying scientist? There were geniuses who didn't think their intelligence made them better than everyone else. Yet Smith couldn't gripe at OSRD. It had been the slimmest of pickings.

American scientists had analyzed debriefing records of every Allied aircrew that reported an encounter with Foo Fighters, the interrogations of every German POW that claimed knowledge of them, all known photos, and standard-speed film footage obtained on gun cameras and precursors to the current mission. Top scientists at the Manhattan District Project had even been consulted, to no avail.

Elite scientists disagreed about Foo Fighters. Some felt they were not aircraft, but rather ball lightning, free-floating plasmas, piezoelectric effects, or other electromagnetic phenomena. Other scientists felt that some Foo Fighters had to be physical objects. Esoteric speculations such as the extraterrestrial hypothesis were rejected.

Whatever the truth, Doctor Bush, Doctor Hunsaker, and the other ten members of OSRD's Majestic Twelve Special Studies Group wanted empirical confirmation. They were insistent that an airborne Foo Fighter be viewed in the wild by an expert in high-voltage electromagnetism. There was a narrow pool of such physicists, especially those who didn't need glasses. Glasses fogged, and a nerd wearing coke bottles didn't have eyesight acute enough for aircraft observation. The pool of genius, high-voltage physicists with fighter-pilot vision was dishearteningly small.

That pool was drained dry by the Manhattan District Project. Doctor Oppenheimer, its lead scientist, was adamant that top Manhattan Engineering District scientists such as Bohr, Fermi, Compton, and Schwinger were irreplaceable assets it would be unconscionable to risk in combat. General Groves, who had operational control of the Manhattan District Project, had flipped his wig at the suggestion that a scientist with direct knowledge of it be sent on a bombing run. If the bomber were downed, the physicist might be captured by the Nazis, interrogated, and compromise the Manhattan District Project irreparably.

An additional problem was the unwillingness of cowardly intellectuals to risk their lives. In the entire United States, there were but a few dozen genius-level physicists who specialized in high-voltage electromagnetism, had perfect vision, and had not worked on the Manhattan District Project. However, none were willing to play German roulette and go on bomber runs.

Except Devlin.

"Going to start recording Doctor," Smith said. "You ready?"

Devlin nodded.

"Not trying to patronize you," Smith said, "but just so we're clear. This recording is to convey your observations in case you don't make it back alive. I need you to be as detailed as possible, within reason. We do have time constraints."

"Could you radio the Luftwaffe and have them delay attack until my analysis is complete?"

"Convince the Kraut Balls to stop jamming our radios and I'd be happy to. Though I worry the Nazis may lack empathy for our plight."

Smith pressed the green button. The small green light above it lit, indicating the recorder was operational.

"You are the first Allied physicist to personally observe a Foo Fighter," Smith said. "What is your assessment?"

Devlin peered at the Foo Fighters a long moment. He then looked at Smith with great intensity, but there was also something distant in his expression. Devlin peered back out at the Foo Fighters.

"I was one of those scientists of the opinion that most Foo Fighters were probably ball lightning or some other electromagnetic phenomenon," Devlin said. "I still believe many Foo Fighter sightings were probably ball lightning. Should I survive the bombing run, I have pertinent observations about ball lightning which I shall proffer on the return flight. For now, I will focus on our seminal discovery that Foo Fighters are physical aircraft. Many scientists have postulated this fact, or presumed it, myself included, but this expedition has proven it."

Devlin summarized the expedition's initial sighting of Foo Fighters, their rapid acceleration towards *Bachelor's Den*, and their instantaneous deceleration.

"Any conventional aircraft," Devlin said, "would be destroyed by such rapid accelerations and decelerations and the resultant forces. Unless severe time dilation is occurring or the conventional laws of mechanics as we understand them do not apply for some reason."

Devlin summarized the way rounds fired at the periphery of the Foo Fighters circled around them rather than continuing in a straight line and contacting them.

"This behavior," Devlin said, "is analogous to light deflecting around a star due to gravitation. The craft appear to be generating gravitational fields and operating in their own relativistic frame of reference, even though the notion of absolute relativism may itself be fallacious."

Devlin held his hand on the tip of his chin and oxygen mask and tapped his fingers rapidly, as if sending Morse code.

"All objects generate gravitational fields proportional to their mass," Devlin said, "but Foo Fighters appear to be generating gravitational forces far in excess of those expected given their apparent mass, even if they are presumed to be homogenous solids comprised of the densest elements in the periodic table. The objects cannot be homogenous solids however, as they must contain internal propulsion componentry generating their artificial gravitation."

Devlin summarized the downing of the Foo Fighters, and emphasized the fact that spherical or semispherical objects were observed within the undulating external sheath, which he referred to as a plasma.

"Given the work on this matter by other specialists, one Navy radar and magnetic expert in particular, the symmetrical shape of the Foo Fighters was mildly surprising. A craft with pronounced asymmetry was expected. It may be that internal components of the craft exhibit the expected asymmetry, or that a different method of achieving the postulated polarization, such as toroids, has been employed."

Devlin's fingers began tapping more frenetically on his chin, like the wings of a hummingbird, so fast a Fastax would be needed to discern them.

"It could also be that the Foo Fighter achieves asymmetry by utilizing a concentric spherical capacitive configuration. If so, dielectrics with exceptionally high K-values would be expected inside the craft between concentricities. Study of these high-K dielectrics might be rewarding."

Smith found Devlin's remarks fascinating yet confusing. He listened intently, trying to understand as much as he could, while Devlin droned on like one of the bomber engines.

25

Devlin was still droning on. He described the way the Foo Fighters had stalled aircraft engines and jammed radios.

"The Foo Fighters generate potent electromagnetic fields and forces," he said. "These fields and forces appear to impede the functioning of electric devices on nearby objects via induction. Though this is one of the most baffling aspects of Foo Fighter performance to uneducated layperson bomber crews, it is completely explained by extant conventional theory, especially Maxwell's equations. The spikes of ammeters observed by the pilot, copilot, radioman, and engineer are proof of electromagnetic induction."

McGinnon approached, sweating profusely. He stood before Smith and waited.

"Enclosing aircraft engines and other electromagnetic devices in Faraday cages may provide defense against inductive effects," Devlin said, "though this hardening comes at the expense of significant weight increases and commensurate decreases in fuel efficiency and range. Should the Nazis develop more robust versions of Foo Fighters which create inductive interference of greater magnitude, as is feared, Faraday cages or other inductive countermeasures may become mandatory on all aircraft."

As Smith unplugged from the small customized interphone, he envisioned LeMay, Eisenhower, and Marshall listening to Devlin's assessment and groaning at the prospect of retrofitting tens of thousands of aircraft. Smith plugged into the normal interphone system.

"Bearing and range, Captain Ostrye," Forrest said. "We're about twenty five minutes from IP."

"Let's start donning those flak jackets and helmets," Ostrye said. "Jerry'll crash the party anytime now. Clear your masks, keep your eyes peeled like spuds, and be sharp on those Brownings. Call your fighters out and no shouting."

"Sorry to interrupt, Captain Ostrye," Smith said. "I'll just be a moment. You read me on the interphone McGinnon?"

McGinnon flipped open his oxygen mask.

"Course I read you," he said, "I'm standing right in front of you."

"I wanna keep everyone in the loop," Smith said.

"Sure you do," Gassoway said.

"Cameras all secured in the LVADs. Everything triple checked. No FUBARs." McGinnon brandished a jovial smile. "Who designed that bomb bay walkway? Ringling Brothers?" McGinnon laughed. "Felt like I was walking a goddamn tightrope."

"Same clowns that designed my turret," Tucker said.

"Ringling Brothers," Smith said, "would have installed a safety net."

"What about the last Fastax?" McGinnon said.

"Keeping it in reserve in the nose," Smith said. "On the off chance something else amazing transpires."

"Off chance my ass," Gassoway said.

"Haven't seen much action in the nose," McGinnon said. "Sure you don't want the last camera in the waist gun window?"

"I love the camera right where it is up front," the pudgy photographer said. "So we don't have to move it."

"I'm not lazy," McGinnon said. "And I see the wisdom of keeping a camera in reserve. But wouldn't it make more sense to place the final camera where we've seen all the action so far?"

"The final camera," Smith said, "is right where I want it."

To be continued. . .

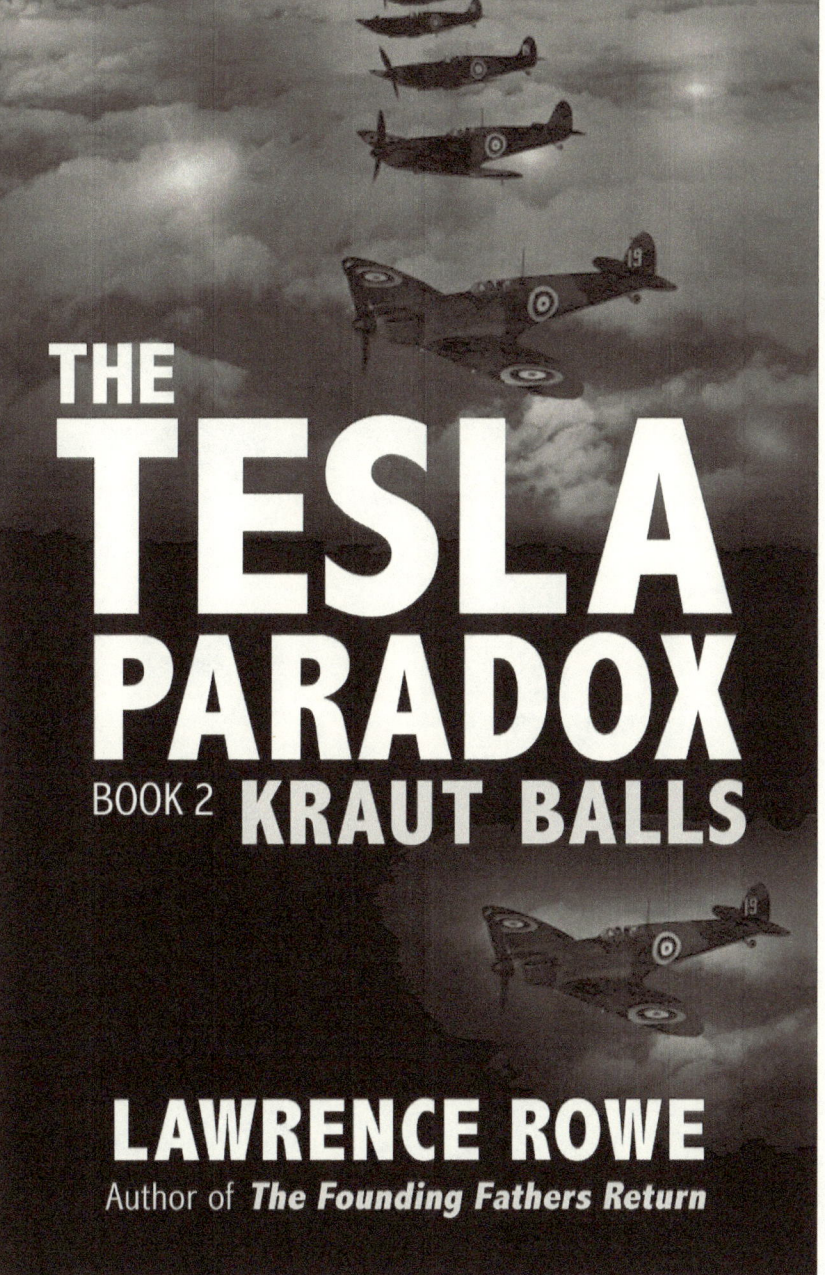

THE
TESLA
PARADOX
BOOK 2 KRAUT BALLS

LAWRENCE ROWE
Author of *The Founding Fathers Return*

Visit LawrenceRowe.com to learn more about
The Tesla Paradox 2: Kraut Balls.

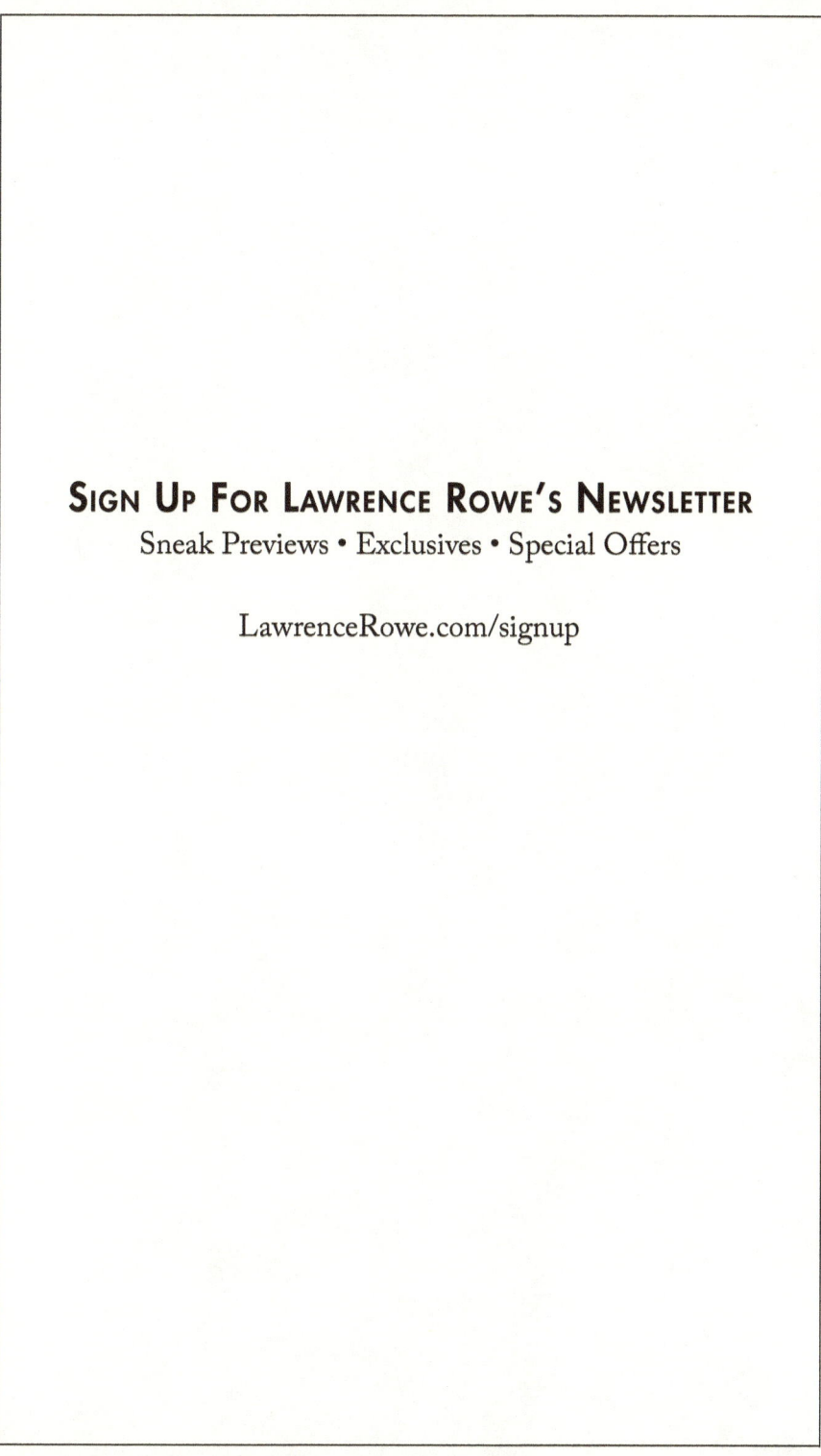

Some men would be great in any time.

THE
FOUNDING
FATHERS
RETURN
A Novel

LAWRENCE ROWE

Visit LawrenceRowe.com to learn more about
The Founding Fathers Return.

THE FOUNDING FATHERS RETURN

A Novel